LUCKY COLOR

LUCKY BREAK SERIES

HOPE MALONE

Copyright © 2023 by Andrene Low writing as Hope Malone.
Bad Birds is a branch (some might say twig) of Squabbling
Sparrows Press. All rights reserved.

ISBN #978-1-7386068-1-8

No part of this book may be reproduced in any form or by any
electronic or mechanical means, including information storage
and retrieval systems, without written permission from the author
or publisher, except for brief quotations in a book review.

A catalogue record of the paperback version of this title is
available from the National Library of New Zealand.

ONE

DAISY

The sun peeking through the partially closed shutters wakes me with a start. For a moment I think I've slept-in, but a check of the antique alarm clock on my bedside table eases my fears.

I don't have time to lie here luxuriating. After stretching my arms above my head, I shake off the remnants of sleep.

I've got forty-five minutes before I have to open The Daisy Chain, my flower shop, and the culmination of years of hard work. It represents both my independence and determination to build something of my own.

There are some who'd call me stubborn, especially my parents. To them, it made no sense when I could as easily have stayed working at the family's nursery and flower shop in Taylor's Mistake further down the coast.

Showered and dressed in my uniform of oft-washed jeans and a dark blue t-shirt with an embroidered daisy on the front, I skip downstairs. In a practiced move, I swipe my hand up the wall, flipping the shop lights on and illuminating the cozy space. After opening the back door to a small courtyard beyond, I zigzag the length of the shop.

I'm not idle on my way, checking on the buckets of flowers as I pass. My flowers are always fresh—I wouldn't have it any other way. There are a few I'll need to weed out, with them wilting despite my having added flower food to the water to help prolong the blooms.

With the bolts top and bottom unlocked, I swing the front door wide and slide a garden gnome in place to stop it from slamming shut.

I'm soon rewarded with a sea breeze that, after filling the shop, finds its way out the back door.

Without this rough-and-ready air-conditioning, I'd risk heat exhaustion at the height of summer. And while the hottest time of year is still a month or two away, today feels like it'll be warm.

To help offset the cloying heat, I breathe deeply, enjoying the ozone wafting through the air. It's the last respite I get with my first customer arriving seconds later.

It's Mrs. Jefferson, in for her usual Friday bouquet of whatever is bright and cheerful. More regulars follow, with me never getting more than a few minutes to myself.

By the end of the day, my fingers are battered and stained from the stems and thorns, and my back aches from constantly being on my feet, but I'm content. As well as my regular orders, I've made up colorful bouquets, all ready for the Saturday morning rush.

Slowly, but surely, I'm becoming known for my unique arrangements. It's something that has even seen me arranging flowers for weddings up at Maddigan's, the flashiest hotel in town. My determination is paying off, with the shop thriving.

Dusk is falling over Coogan's Break when I flip the shop sign to CLOSED. However, the front window glowing with warmth, I don't yet close the door.

Rather, I'm drawn outside for a final breath of fresh air and time to revel in my accomplishments. Life is good, with one exception. I've got no-one to share it with, unlike many of my friends.

It's certainly meant a lot of matchmaking on their parts, although without success to date. Yep, my *success to date* has been woeful, with Thursday night a case in point.

I'm up even earlier the following morning, well before the sun blinds me. The weather forecast being as optimistic as it is, I open the shutters, and even the windows of my little apartment wide. After taking in my sliver of a sea view, I breathe deeply, the air heavy with the scent of possibility.

This morning I'm meeting my BFF, Skye, for coffee and pastries in the courtyard before I open up. We don't get to see each other as often as we used to, with her consumed both with Skye High Pies, her bakery, and Seth, her gorgeous man. None of this mattered, with our friendship as strong as ever.

As with every other morning of the working week, I grab a fresh pair of jeans and a clean navy-blue t-shirt with a requisite embroidered daisy on the front.

It's not by accident I've chosen these items as my uniform. Apart from being practical, I know they flatter my curves. It's the generous nature of these that often has people underestimating how capable I am, and with good reason.

Hours spent on my feet in concert with moving heavy buckets of flowers, and there's more to me than meets the eye.

I'm not idle while I wait for Skye to arrive, knowing she can't be far away. The woman is rarely late thanks to years of starting her working day at 4am. I'm about to flick on the shop lights when I notice someone waiting out front.

The shop hours are clearly posted and so, keeping a low profile, I slip out the back door without them seeing me. While I'm serious about The Daisy Chain, I'm also deadly serious about anything Skye will turn up with. She's the queen of yummy baked goods and wonderful coffee.

I've hardly settled at the little wrought-iron patio set when her signature pale pink hatchback pulls up behind my canary yellow 4x4.

A moment later, she deposits a brown paper bag and two takeaway coffees in a cardboard holder on the small table. "I hope you're hungry. The new girl messed up the icing on a batch of red velvet cupcakes."

Rather than appear annoyed about this mishap, her eyes are twinkling with merriment as she flicks her ponytail out of the way. Skye is all warmth and laughter, and the perfect balance to my more determined nature.

After checking the writing on the lids of the coffees, I grab the one with almond milk. Not that I'm lactose intolerant, but that I like the nutty flavor. The first sip is like a gift from the gods, with me putting my cup back down with a heartfelt sigh. "You're a lifesaver."

Likewise, Skye is busy with her coffee, although not for long. She's soon ripping open the brown bakery bag to reveal cupcakes that look as though they've been sent from New York with insufficient postage.

It's not until we've both helped ourselves, and taken big bites, that silence falls, even if this doesn't last. While the cupcakes might look like a disaster, there's nothing wrong with the taste, and there's nothing I can do to squelch my moan of pleasure.

I'm still licking my fingers when Skye eyeballs me, her fiery curls shining in the early morning light. "Okay, spill! Tell me everything about your date Thursday night."

I take a moment to think about how I respond. It was Skye who'd set me up with Leonard from the bookshop further down the street. She's got a vested interest in the outcome, meaning I need to let her down gently.

"It was nice. We had a lot to talk about." And this is true, even if I've had more animated conversations at Chamber of Commerce meetings. I should have known I was in trouble when he said his favorite author was James Joyce, following it up with an expression that was pure fan boy.

"And?" Skye prompts. "Don't leave out any details!"

"Well, he walked me home and kissed me goodnight."

I'd usually be fanning myself as Skye is now, but there's no need. Honestly, the encounter had been about as exciting as kissing my little brother on the cheek when he graduated from middle school. I'd had to lean down then, too.

Across the small table, Skye has a dreamy look on her face. "This is so romantic! When are you seeing him again?"

"Yeah, about that..." I don't have time to continue, with someone hammering on the front door. A quick look at my watch and I'm surprised to see that it's past opening time. It's always this way when Skye and I get together. Somehow, time flies by.

"Hey, I'd better get going." We're both on our feet when I decide I can't leave things as they are. "Skye, can you... Can you please not set me up with anyone else? It's just that..."

This time, the knocking is even louder. "I'll tell you more when I can, but, yeah, no more dates, please."

There's no missing that I've upset my friend. Her face is a picture of dejection. Her heart is in the right place, but the men she keeps setting me up with just don't do it for me. I'll make it up to her, but I can't go through another blind date. They're just too demoralizing.

I'd rather imagine there's a man out there for me than go on a series of dates and prove there isn't. And I know I'm being petty in wanting a man who's taller than my five-foot-eight, but there you go.

Is it wrong to want to wear heels when I go out on a date?

I'm sliding the bolts on the front door to the side when I realize that rather than it being a customer, it's my landlord. The door isn't even fully open when he barges past me. Honestly, as well as being a complete sleazeball, the guy needs to learn some manners.

It's like this every time he visits, with him never telling me in advance that he'll be calling by. However, today's visit isn't totally unexpected, not with my lease on the building up for renewal. And, sure enough, he's brandishing an updated lease, the paper rustling as he waves it under my nose. The pungency of his cologne suffocating as I skim read the document.

To a background of his huffing and puffing, a knot forms in my stomach. It's one that tightens with every clause and sub-clause.

However, the rent increase that he's slipped in like a thief in the night toward the end has the knot looking more like a noose. While it was probably illegal for him to almost double my rent as he's proposing, it was no surprise coming from this guy.

"I'm not signing this. This is extortion!"

Even though I've stood up for myself, there's no missing that my voice is shaking with anger and fear, with him immediately latching onto this. While his eyebrows had initially shot up in surprise, he's not backing down.

"Well, pretty lady, I'm sure we can work out some way for you to pay what you can afford."

He'd hit on me before, but this time, I snap, itching to wipe that nasty smile off his face. My heart pounding, I draw myself up to my full height, taking delight in looking down at him.

"Well, Mr. Walker, you know what you can do with your rent hike?!"

While I doubt what I have in mind is physically possible, I'd pay to see him try. Unfortunately, with the lease due to expire the following day, he'd then taken great delight in evicting me.

And while this was probably as illegal as the rent increase, there wasn't a lot I could do about it on a Saturday morning.

"Anything I find on the premises on Monday morning, I'll sell to offset my costs. Do I make myself clear?"

It was because of this, I'd had the sale to end all sales, finishing the day with not a flower to my name. It's also something that soon has me perched precariously atop my little stepladder, armed with a kitchen knife instead of a screwdriver.

No way was I leaving my wonderful sign with its hand-painted daisies behind for my deadbeat landlord to destroy. I've only loosened one screw when a mixture of musk and sandalwood surrounds me, and the hairs on the back of my neck prick up.

On sensing movement directly behind me, I turn to see what's going on and come close to falling off my perch. Oh my, one look at this guy and the tingling in my neck heads south and I have to swallow, although only after licking my lips.

Dark brown hair, tousled by the wind, frames a rugged face adorned with a full beard. Clad in jeans and a fitted white t-shirt, my pulse quickens in response to his aura of strength.

"Lady, you are an accident waiting to happen."

Holy moly, if I thought my girly bits were on fire before, it's nothing compared to when the rumble of his voice cuts right through me. Why couldn't Skye have set me up with a guy like this rather than that book nerd, Leonard?

Then my dreams come crashing down. First off, a guy this hot would never want to saddle himself with someone as boring as me. And if I was brave enough to go on a date, I wouldn't have a clue how to act.

How would you even flirt with someone like this? Anything beyond shy glances and I'm lost. And I suspect this guy would want a lot more than those. Never mind want, he'd probably demand it.

. . .

When the stepladder wobbles thanks to my being off balance, it's only him steadying me that stops me from taking a nasty fall. His hands rest gently on my hips, with my gaze drawn to his intricate tattoos.

They swirl the length of his arms before disappearing under the sleeves of his t-shirt, leaving me breathless. The dark blues and greens, with splashes of red, contrast with his olive skin, further adding to his dangerous allure.

As he helps me down, the designs come alive, twisting and turning with the muscles in his arms, making me acutely aware of his raw, untamed energy. It's only when I'm safely down on the sidewalk that I realize just how tall he is.

While I might like my flowers to be sweetness and light, I prefer my men much darker. Of course, I'm not brave enough to share this dirty little secret with my girlfriends.

TWO

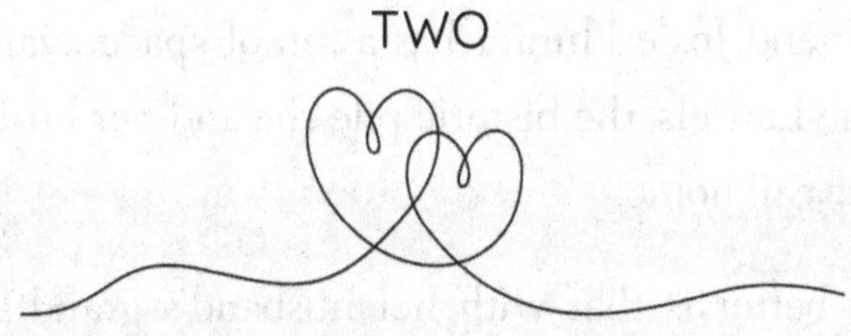

DAISY

After helping me remove the sign from above the front door of my shop, the hunk had disappeared as suddenly as he'd appeared. It was as if he was a figment of my fevered imagination.

My mind is crowded with who he was and where he'd come from. This has me hardly aware of what I'm doing. As consumed as I've been with thoughts of what the guy would look like naked, it's not until much later that I finally face the challenges ahead.

As easy as it would be to hire a truck and move back home, I don't want to. I've worked too hard to establish myself in Coogan's Break to give up that easily. It's then I have a brainwave.

My friend Josie Hunter has a ton of space available at The Laurels, the historic pile she and her husband Chase call home.

Even better is that with her husband's grandfather having moved into a retirement home, the apartment over the triple-car-garage is empty. While only a temporary fix, it would at least give me some breathing space until I can sort something else out.

The relief when she says she and Chase will even help me move the next day is immeasurable. The last thing I do before I head upstairs for the night is to check my bank account. It was a habit I'd gotten into when I first started in business, and one I don't seem able to abandon.

It's on seeing the balance that I give thought to a move that would avoid me needing to worry about a landlord ever again. Or am I simply dreaming about that as I had been about my mystery man?

After moving into the apartment at Josie and Chase's, I'd spent days combing the listings for a commercial space that suited my budget.

Unfortunately, without a lot of luck. Actually, make that without ANY luck.

Anything I viewed that was walk-in ready was so over my budget as to make my eyes water. It was also something that had me giving the realtor a piece of my mind. Why he insisted on showing me premises I couldn't afford was beyond me, explaining to him that this was wasting my time, and his.

Budget-busters aside, the rest had proven to be too big, or too far from downtown. Friday morning, with desperation nipping at my heels, I'd spotted a run-down Victorian for sale on Beach Road.

The two-story building had seen better days, with paint peeling on the siding and a sagging front porch. However, it was the perfect size, only a block from my current location, and, best of all, I could live upstairs.

Perhaps the most appealing feature of the old building was that it had been a shop in the past, right down to double doors on the corner. These faced the intersection it sat on.

As well as passing traffic, it would also be easier for customers to park right outside when they were collecting their flowers.

Perfect enough that I'd rung the realtor immediately and waited for her to swing by so I could see if the inside was salvageable. After she'd unlocked the front door with a creak, I'd stepped inside, a puff of dust swirling around my ankles.

But beyond the grime and cobwebs, I could see potential. The large front windows, when cleaned, would let in plenty of natural light. The wood floors were solid, and the basic layout would work well for a flower shop.

Best of all was that the price was a steal. Cheap enough for me to manage the deposit, and if business was as brisk as it had been at my old place, comfortably cover the mortgage repayments. It was exactly the fresh start my business needed.

After an emergency meeting with the loans officer at my bank, I'd signed the papers later that same day. It definitely helped that my folks had agreed to guarantee me for my small mortgage.

Five days after being evicted, and I had a new home and shop, and it was going to be even better than ever. Now all I needed to do was celebrate.

After picking up a bottle of bubbly on the way home, I park out front of the garage at Josie's. Her stepping out the back door of the main house soon after I get out of my car says she's been waiting for me.

As always, she's dressed in vintage fifties clothing, with no one element out of place. It's been the same for as long as I've known her, and if I was to see her dressed any other way, it would feel strange. The retro styles are also the perfect foil for her curves.

"You're looking pleased with yourself."

She's right, with there being a definite spring in my step at knowing my future is secure. "I am. You are looking at the proud owner of the most run-down Victorian in town."

There's no missing her surprise. "You've bought something?!" After shaking her head as if to clear her thoughts, she continues. "I mean, that's fantastic, just unexpected is all."

I have to agree with her on this. It's certainly not something I'd have done in the past, but under all that grime and neglect, the old building had spoken to me.

"I know, it's crazy, right? Now all I need to do is find someone who can renovate it for me."

At my revelation, concern clouds Josie's face. "It's that bad?"

I'm still nodding when she talks again, although it's nothing about renovations.

"Hey, join us for dinner tonight. We can celebrate your new shop."

To the casual observer, it'd be a lovely invitation, but with Josie and Chase often laughing at inside jokes and shared glances, it could make for an awkward dinner. My love life was miserable enough, without having bliss like theirs rubbed in my face.

As if sensing my reticence, she presses on. "Chase's grandfather is coming over, and he loves meeting new people. Please say yes!"

Given Mr. Hunter Senior will be there, it should be okay. I also don't fancy spending my Friday night drinking alone. "I'd love to. Just let me get changed. Six o'clock, okay?"

That evening, I knock on the back door, looking forward to dinner. I'm holding the bottle of bubbly, which I hand to Josie when she opens the door.

On stepping inside, the familiar warmth of her home envelopes me. The cozy living room is adorned with flickering candles, while soft music plays in the background. The scent of something delicious wafts from the kitchen, making my stomach rumble with anticipation.

I'd worked up quite the appetite over the day.

"Daisy, come on through and meet Chase's grandfather. He's such a character!" She'd then led me through to the dining room, where the table was beautifully set with fine china and sparkling silverware.

The old man was already seated at the head of the table, his presence commanding and full of life. His eyes lit up when he caught sight of me, and he beckoned me to take the seat beside him.

Over the course of the evening, we shared stories and laughter. Mr. Hunter regaled us with tales of Chase, and his brother Ethan, and the trouble they'd gotten into. It was hearing this that had me realizing the old man had actually raised the brothers from when they were young kids.

Where the parents were in all of this, I'm unsure, with any reference to them, noticeably absent. Despite this, I couldn't help but be captivated by the old man's vibrant spirit, with it clear why Chase and Josie loved him so dearly.

Josie has cleared away the dinner plates when I make noises about leaving. "Sorry to leave so early, but I need to get on with researching local contractors." While not exactly a small town, neither is Coogan's Break a bustling city.

I've not pushed my seat back when Josie coughs, causing me to look in her direction. I've known her long enough to know that expression all too well, with it having gotten me into trouble in the past. "What?"

JOSH

I'm with my teammates at Eagles Nest, the beautiful home of Ethan Hunter, my boss, and Lindsey, his wife. We're enjoying our regular Friday night drinks.

Of the Lucky Break Construction crew, only Ethan, Malakai Everhart, Cole Silverman, and Daemon Booth, are still here. Heath, my brother, is out of town, which I'm okay with, the constant reminders of the hand I've been dealt, difficult at the best of times.

As for all the others, they've headed home to their partners.

I'd be all for that myself, but I'm single, and the longer I can put off heading home to an empty house, the better. It's a thought that has me remembering the woman I'd helped with her sign.

She'd appealed to me in a big way. Big enough that I'd even driven by on the Monday when I knew the shop would be open again. Only it wasn't, nor would it ever be again, with a big FOR LEASE sign in the window.

If I had someone like her in my life, I wouldn't currently be contemplating getting a dog, or even a cat. Even a blasted goldfish would be better than walking into a house devoid of all life.

A house devoid of any color, thanks to the condition I'd inherited from my dad. It was one I was stuck with and that my brother delights in telling all and sundry that he'd avoided.

The conversation shifts, becoming more serious when Ethan is asked about any future projects. Normally, by this point, we'd have heard what was coming up, with projects overlapping.

Rather than respond as he usually would, Ethan remains tight-lipped, leaving us all in the dark. This doesn't altogether worry me, happy to have a break from the frenetic pace we've been keeping. I also know he'll move heaven and earth to keep us fully employed and busy.

There's a lot more to Lucky Break Construction than just building stuff. Part of the reason Ethan had set the company up was to help guys like himself. Guys who'd screwed up their lives by mixing with the wrong sort, or just by being young and stupid.

However, when Ethan eventually blurts out that he might have to let go of some casual workers, my easygoing demeanor fades.

Lost in my thoughts, I take a sip of my beer, contemplating the uncertain future that looms before us. I'm still weighing up my options when Lindsey's phone rings, interrupting the heavy silence.

There's no missing the smile when she sees who's calling, with her immediately excusing herself to go inside and take the call. On her return shortly after, her face is alive with excitement and mischief.

"Guess what, guys?" Lindsey announces, her eyes sparkling playfully. "I might have stumbled upon your next project, and it's a doozy!"

I'm taking this at face value until her gaze lands on me, the speculation somewhat unsettling. Why do I feel I'm being set up? Perhaps because it's something that happens all too often.

I can't remember how many times I've been sent to buy paint, despite my saying over and over that it's not a good idea.

"Come on, sweetheart, spill!" Ethan's prompt is enough to have her abandoning her assessment of me, and turning to the others.

To a man, we wait to hear more about this surprise project, and despite her strange examination earlier, I can't help but feel a surge of excitement. The team thrives on challenges, and the prospect of something unusual is like a shot of adrenaline.

"It's different from what we usually do." Lindsey's voice brims with enthusiasm, only adding to the allure of what she's about to reveal. "It's a shop fit-out, but I'm sure it's nothing you can't handle."

It's when Lindsey reveals the address of the potential project that my heart skips a beat. I know that address intimately, like the rhythm of my heartbeat, and memories surge, taking me back to a time long ago.

"Are you okay, Josh?" There's no missing the concern in Lindsey's eyes.

I have to clear my throat before I can respond, a mixture of excitement, nostalgia, and apprehension close to overwhelming me. "Ah, it's nothing. Was just thinking about something, is all."

Mindful of everyone staring while waiting for me to expand, memories crowd my mind, intertwined with the present. Could it be fate has intervened to have me back at the very place I'd last felt normal?

A place where my being colorblind hadn't mattered, to where I'd first learned there was more to life than color.

As the evening at Ethan and Lindsey's house wound down, I bid farewell to my teammates and made my way home. The drive felt longer than usual, the silence of the empty house that awaited me weighing heavily.

It was a mix of exhaustion and restlessness that had me looking through some old photo albums. As I flipped through the pages, my heart swelled with both joy and a tinge of sorrow.

There they were, my grandparents, standing proudly in front of their shop, beaming with love and passion. And there, in the middle, was a younger version of myself, filled with innocence and curiosity. But one thing stood out—my brother Heath was missing from these precious snapshots.

A wave of sadness washed over me as I traced the lines of the photographs with my fingertips. I couldn't help but be reminded of the incident that had forever changed the course of my childhood.

It was during a local gridiron game when my color blindness unknowingly became a hindrance. In my eyes, the colors of the two teams were indistinguishable, with me as likely to pass the ball to the opposing team as I was to my own.

That moment marked a turning point, as I was deemed unfit for future team sports and activities. The hard shell I'd formed protected me from the nasty comments that followed.

Meanwhile, Heath reveled in the fact he'd escaped inheriting the defective gene. It was something that had him training with his team the day the photo of me and our grandparents was taken.

As I gazed at those images, a mix of anger and longing coursed through me. I couldn't change my eyesight, but I could change the narrative it had created in my life.

The opportunity to restore my grandparents' old shop offered a glimmer of hope—a chance to rewrite that painful chapter, to find acceptance and belonging once again.

With a renewed sense of purpose, I closed the photo album and made a vow to myself. The upcoming project would not only be about transforming the physical space, it would be about reclaiming a part of myself that had been overshadowed by shame and exclusion.

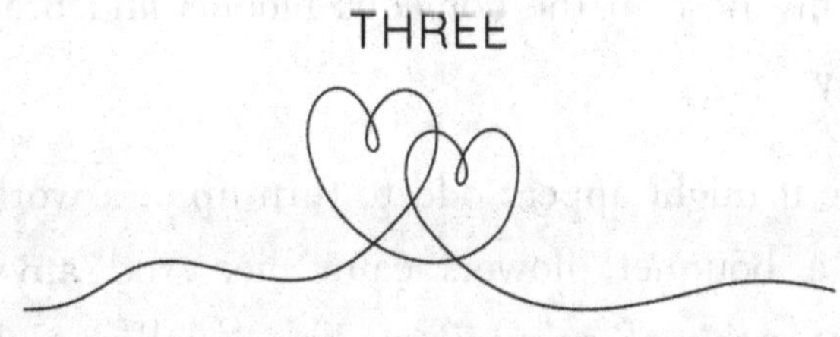

THREE

DAISY

As I stand on the threshold of my new shop, my heart races thanks to an interesting mix of anticipation and bone-deep dread.

The very thought of the challenges ahead has me in danger of crushing the bouquet I'm holding, with this vision of beauty at odds with my outfit.

Fully expecting to pitch in and help the Lucky Break Construction team where I can, I've come dressed for action. This sees me in my oldest jeans, boots, and a cherry pink t-shirt that's riddled with holes.

It's not how I'd usually dress, but suits my plans for the day. To calm my nerves at being seen like this, I bury my nose in the gorgeous blooms and breathe deeply.

While it might appear odd to turn up at a worksite with a bouquet, flowers calm me. And anyway, they're nothing fancy, with me having collected them from the garden at Josie's. California poppies for their vibrant orange, and lilacs for their heavenly scent.

They immediately work their magic, my senses numbed to my current state and the misery that surrounds me. The worn-out building, with its faded façade and cracked windows, hints at tales of neglect and forgotten dreams.

On stepping inside, my eyes widen. I don't remember the building being this awful the day I'd viewed it, committing to the purchase only six hours later. However, it had been a bright sunny day on that occasion.

Today, dust particles hang lifeless in any beams of sunlight strong enough to pierce through the filthy windows. The air is musty in stark contrast to the vibrant scents that will soon fill the air.

Eventually, my gaze drifts to the peeling floral wallpaper, with its pattern from a bygone era. It must have been glorious in its day. Now it's faded to a depressing mishmash of blooms that have long since been mulched into obscurity.

Next to catch my attention are the scuffed wooden floors and the sagging ceiling, with the state of them having doubt washing over me. I knew from the start that transforming this dilapidated space would be a daunting task.

However, it's one I'm up for, never again wanting to be at the mercy of an unscrupulous landlord. I don't care how many hours I have to work; I'm making a go of this. Never let it be said Daisy Green backed down from a challenge.

While my focus is to get the shop ready to open, I'm also keen on tidying up the living quarters upstairs. Even though Josie and Chase are okay about me staying, I know how quickly that can sour. I'd like to be out before it gets to the stage that they think I'm breathing too loudly.

My steps determined, I traverse the shop, my fingers grazing the chipped edges of the counters original to the old place. My sunny disposition soon takes over and I'm able to envision the shelves lined with beautiful vases and a kaleidoscope of blooms.

When I close my eyes, I can even see their bright hues intermingling and infusing the air with a symphony of fragrances. It's when I open the door at the back of the shop that my upbeat dreams come crashing down.

Once in the narrow hallway, I'm surrounded by a murky rabbit-warren of rooms. When a bead of sweat crawls spider-like down my back, there's nothing I can do to stop the shudder that wracks my frame.

The grand opening being less than a month away, the clock was ticking. Even leaving the back rooms for later, the task ahead is still a major challenge. I need the Lucky Break Construction crew here to breathe life into my vision.

Minutes stretch into an eternity as I anxiously await their arrival. They can't be too far off with a bright yellow dumpster already sitting out front in readiness for the inevitable demolition.

Finally, the sound of heavy boots and the rumble of deep voices signals their arrival, and my heart skips a beat as anticipation coils within me.

Ethan Hunter, the company owner, and Josie's brother-in-law, strides into the shop. He's backed up by half-a-dozen guys who leave me lost for words and a little breathless. While I knew Ethan was good-looking, I hadn't realized the same was true of his team.

We're talking about the construction industry's answer to Chippendales. Give these boys some pants that Velcroed up the sides, and they'd be all set.

"Morning, Ms. Green!" Ethan's bright greeting is followed by a warm smile, with this backed up by others on the team. "We're ready to get cracking." He then puts a copy of the plan we'd agreed upon, down on the counter next to me.

A glance at it has me swallowing at the magnitude of the project. "There's a lot to be done. Are you sure you'll be able to manage everything in time for the official opening?" I'm then quick to add, "And please, call me Daisy."

Ethan nods, his eyes scanning the room. "We'll make it happen ... Daisy. We've seen worse than this, trust me."

It's an observation that's met with knowing laughter by the team and even a muttered, "Hell yes!" from one of them.

I then watch as the crew members, each one more attractive than the last, assess the space, occasionally stopping to check the plan. Their camaraderie is clear as they exchange playful banter and chuckles.

When they split up, determined to get as much done as possible, I can't help but feel a glimmer of hope. And then the shop darkens, with it not taking me long to see why.

The man in the doorway is enormous, but definitely in a good way. However, it's not until he steps inside the shop that I realize I know him, even if only in passing. It doesn't matter that our time together had been brief. There isn't a chance I'd forget a man like this.

There's something about him that tugs at my heartstrings. Okay, and other bits, if I'm being brutally honest. There's a familiarity about him that has nothing to do with him helping me take the sign down at my old shop.

Rather, it's as if we knew each other in another lifetime. Try as I might, I can't put my finger on it, even if I'd like to. Oh, my lord, would I ever.

I'm only conscious I'm using my bouquet like a fan when a couple of petals come loose and flutter to the wooden floorboards.

"Sheesh, Kendrick! Do you think you could turn up on time for once?"

There'd been no missing the exasperation in Ethan's voice before he disappeared out back. There'd also been what I think was resignation, as though he knows this guy will never be on time.

Not that the new arrival heeds the admonishment. Instead, my mystery man stalks across the shop, leaving me frozen. On him stopping in front of me, I couldn't move if I wanted to.

"Really, you shouldn't have. Brown's my favorite color."

As before, his deep voice vibrates through my body, sending shivers down my spine, leaving me in a daze.

I'm also wondering what he means about brown being his favorite color, when he tips his head toward me. On realizing he's talking about the bouquet I'm gripping like a lifeline, I'm even more confused. Brown? What was he talking about?

There's no missing his eyes sparkling mischievously, with a matching smile playing on lips I long to kiss. I can imagine them plundering my mouth and leaving me begging for more.

His gruff exterior fades away, replaced by a gentleness that draws me in. It also exerts a magnetic pull I know will be dangerous. And yet, isn't that part of his appeal?

I've always played it safe in life, at least where men were concerned. Me telling my old landlord what he could do with his rent increase was in stark contrast. Despite this deviation, I've landed on my feet, although as I stare up, up, up at the man I now know as Josh, I can think of positions I'd prefer.

Even glazed over as I am with thoughts of how this would pan out, there's no missing the sparkle in his eyes dying. Damn it, I should have tamped down my reaction.

Hadn't mom warned me not to wear my heart on my sleeve, to keep something in reserve? It's far too late for this, although I still do my best to squelch my arousal in response to this gorgeous hunk of a man.

"I guess I'd better go get my orders." After a quick look at the plan, he adds, "Daisy Green."

I'm doing everything I can to control my response when he pats me on my arm. He follows this up with a grin that promises more than I'd know what to do with.

While his gesture was casual, there's nothing languid about the electricity that zaps from where he'd touched me to where it shouldn't. As surprising as this has been, it leaves me struggling to keep my composure.

It doesn't take me long to realize that keeping my body under control around this man is a hopeless exercise.

JOSH

As always, I'm last to the site, my preference being to arrive in one piece and not in an ambulance.

Experience has taught me that unless I pay close attention to the traffic signals, things can rapidly turn pear-shaped, especially my truck.

I've hardly stepped inside the shop through the double doors on the corner of the building when I get grief from Ethan. It doesn't matter that he knows why I'm late.

It's as if he feels he has to reprimand me to stop anyone else from getting any ideas about being tardy. After delivering his rebuke, he disappears through the door at the back of the shop.

After brushing his criticism to one side, I cast around. I want to meet the woman crazy enough to take on this project. My history with the shop has me more aware than anyone else on the team, exactly what a money pit it is.

It was why grandpa retired early, selling the building and his sewing machine repair business as a going concern. While he could see fewer people were making their own clothes, the new owners couldn't. They hadn't lasted more than a year before they went out of business.

There followed a jumble of businesses trying to make a go of it, with none succeeding. Given there's little to no foot traffic in this part of town, I reckon the new owner will be as likely to fail.

It was thanks to this that the shop and living quarters had been empty for years now, and doubtless why they're as dilapidated as they are. It wouldn't matter, with the place as monochromatic as any 1960s TV show, at least to my eyes.

Eventually, my memories of sitting out back doing my homework fade, and are replaced by a beacon of vibrancy amidst the desolation of the shop.

I'd recognize those curves anywhere! Haven't I spent the past week fantasizing about them? Her bright personality is reflected in dark blue eyes that hold a fierce determination that I'd already witnessed firsthand.

Her hair is once again tied up in a messy bun as it had been the day that I'd saved her from herself by taking that sign down for her. I can't help but imagine running my fingers through it.

It's a combo that has me crossing the shop without conscious thought. On arriving in front of her, I'm lost for anything sensible to say.

If her physical appeal wasn't dangerous enough, the scent of that bouquet mixed with her own unique perfume has my balls tightening.

Without thinking, I comment on the flowers, unable to avoid a rush of desire as I imagine burying my face in those fragrant blooms. Well, those and her luscious breasts. A man could lose himself in curves like that.

I then watch her going through a million different emotions before finally settling on puzzled. Damn it, I've screwed up again. What on earth possessed me to tell her that brown was my favorite color?

Hadn't I learned my lesson on that front? Apparently not, with the woman's confusion clear. There's also not a chance in hell I'm going near the subject again in order to explain myself.

Instead, I take in the rundown nature of my grandparent's old shop, the memories as strong now as when I'd helped them move out. This woman is delusional if she thinks she'll be opening in a month.

It'd be quicker to bulldoze the place and start again than try to make a silk purse out of this pig's ear. "If you'll excuse me."

After patting her arm, I go in search of Ethan, trying to shake off the memory of her silky-smooth skin. My footsteps echo on the rough floorboards in the hallway, with her unique perfume still clouding my senses.

My imagination is now out of control, with me more focused on what it would be like to run my fingers through her hair than where I'm walking. As my heart races at thoughts of her sheath wrapped tightly around my cock, I smack into the doorframe.

"Damn it, I don't need this."

Lucky for me, there's no-one around to hear me muttering to myself. They already think I've got a screw loose thanks to the number of times I get paint colors wrong.

It's for this reason I'm happier with demo work, and that we'll be demolishing most of the old building isn't in doubt. As for any other plans that Daisy discussed with my boss, who knew?

As I make my way through the building, I eventually find him in what used to be Grannie's office. The musty smell of old books and paper hits me as soon as I walk in. He's holding a sledgehammer, ready to demolish the built-in desk tucked in one corner, and I have to hold myself back from shouting at him to stop.

If I close my eyes, I can still see Grannie sitting at the desk, her pen scratching away at a large, leather-bound ledger. The sound of the pen against the paper echoes in my ears. She never used computers - everything was done by hand.

In contrast to Ethan's air of destruction, the small office is thick with history and nostalgia. On watching him prepare to destroy another piece of my family's history, I have to bite my tongue. I have no say over what stays and what doesn't.

Behind me, Daisy has no compunction in yelling at Ethan to stop what he's doing. "No, you can't demolish that! It's part of the building's charm."

Ethan lowers his sledgehammer to the ground, doing nothing to hide his incredulity. "Charm?"

Ignoring him, Daisy crosses the room and lays her somewhat battered bouquet on the small desk. Thus unencumbered, she grabs a can of spray paint I hadn't noticed sitting on the mantlepiece above the small fireplace, although I recognize it as the brand Ethan uses.

"Unless I mark it with a cross, it is NOT to be demolished. Do I make myself clear?"

Only once Ethan has acknowledged this, does Daisy have a good look at the small room. "Nothing in here is to be touched. Can you please make that clear to your team?"

She gets another nod from Ethan with him walking out into the hallway, and me right behind him. Last to leave is Daisy, with her shutting the door with a resounding bang.

To make doubly sure the room isn't touched, she sprays LEAVE ALONE on the door. This has me pleased the doors are buried beneath half-a-dozen layers of paint rather than raw wood as they'd been in my grandparent's day.

Back then, I could at least admire the natural beauty of the grain.

As I watch this bossy bundle of curves take charge, my senses take a battering. The sound of her no-nonsense boots on the hardwood floors is like music to my ears. The way she moves has my heart racing and my breath quickening.

Blood rushing to my groin has me harder than I've any right to be on a work site. Despite any moral objections my brain might come up with, my body is telling me this is exactly what I want.

FOUR

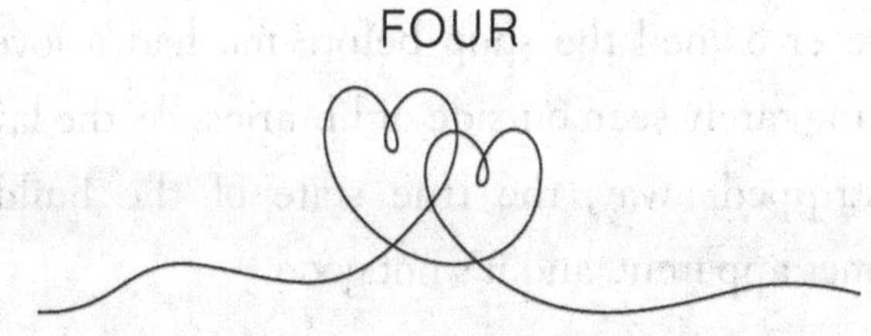

DAISY

It's another half hour before I've marked everything the team can demolish with a large X. It's a lot less than I've been expecting I'd need to get rid of. And I'm okay with that, with it helping both my budget and the timeline.

Only then does Ethan bark orders to his team, his voice booming throughout the building, and the men moving with purpose.

The first thing they do is rip down all the shoddy partition walls, with this making an enormous difference. From there they move onto dismantling worn-out fixtures, and removing any shelving I don't need.

Whoever owned the shop before me had a love of shelving rarely seen outside of libraries. As the layers are stripped away, the true state of the building becomes apparent, and it's not good.

While I'd wanted the Lucky Break team to concentrate on the shop, Ethan had explained it made more sense to complete all the demo in one go. That way, he wouldn't need to hire the dumpster for longer than necessary. And hey, I was all about saving money where I could.

However, the place is in way worse shape than I thought it was when I'd purchased it. And while I've got no construction experience, there's no missing the sound of men sucking air through their teeth. A sure sign they're uncovering horror after horror.

It's nearing the end of the workday, and I'm sitting at the small desk I'd stopped Ethan from demolishing that morning. I'm making notes the old-fashioned way, in a notebook. As much as anything, this allows me to brainstorm my ideas.

I'm tapping my pen against the lined paper, waiting for inspiration when I hear smashing glass from out in the store. What the heck!? I told them I wanted that wavy glass saved.

I'm on my feet a second later, and in the shop, ready to reprimand whoever was responsible. Only the shop is empty. Well, not completely, with there being a couple of large rocks sitting in the middle of the wide plank floors.

Even with no building experience, I know one thing for sure, and that's that the windows hadn't been damaged by anyone on the team. Soon after, I shoot out the front doors, stopping on the edge of the sidewalk and looking wildly about.

I soon spot the delinquents responsible, taking off after the half-dozen kids without a moment's thought. They need to pay for the damage they've caused.

I'm not even close to catching the little devils when I hear footsteps thundering up behind me. A moment later and Josh flies past me, gaining on the kids with impressive speed.

Just as he's taken me by surprise when he raced past, he does the same with the kids, coming to a screeching halt and turning to face them down. I might even feel sorry for them if not for the damage they'd just done to my shop.

If Josh can scare the crap out of them, they might think twice about chucking more rocks through The Daisy Chain's windows. Unfortunately, he's not given the chance, with the kids scattering in all directions.

I'm still having trouble believing their audacity. They had to have known there were people inside when they chucked those rocks.

But as I'd watched them take off, I'd been reminded of my brother's wild days, with him often stirring up trouble with no thought of the consequences.

Upon arrival back at the shop, I get my first proper look at the damage. There's glass everywhere, with shards glittering like forgotten dreams on the wide plank floors.

I'd loved the original glass, knowing that once cleaned, its wavy, handmade distortions would cast gorgeous patterns on the walls of the shop. Now I'll be stuck with something more utilitarian.

After grabbing a broom, I get to work sweeping up. "Those little brats. I loved that glass."

The other thing that annoys me is I'll have to put in an insurance claim to cover the repairs. This has me taking my frustrations out on the broom, soon sweeping the broken glass into a pile in one corner.

In the meantime, Josh, and a guy with an impressive mustache who'd been introduced as Malakai, discuss how they're going to secure the shop. A quick check of the building and it becomes apparent they're the only ones left of the Lucky Break team. The others must have left when I was busy working on my list of things to do.

Despite Malakai being equally blessed in the looks and physique department, he doesn't hold my attention. There's something guarded and edgy about Josh that appeals, even if I'm not sure why.

There's head scratching, and even some dumpster diving, before the pair completes their strategy. This sees them hammering salvaged shelves over the gaping holes. Rather than leave gaps between the boards, they've butted them up against each other, tight enough to even keep the weather out.

Unfortunately, this plunges the shop into darkness with the single bulb hanging high above our heads, not up to lighting the place. Despite knowing the shop will be safe with the windows boarded up, the sooner I can have the glass replaced, the better. The building looks neglected enough as it is, without that in the mix.

It's something that has me calling the only glazier in town that offers an after-hours service. While I wait for my call to be answered, I watch Josh double checking the boards are secure. Of Malakai, there's no sign.

There's an innate beauty in the way Josh moves, how his muscles flex under his fitted t-shirt. And we're talking real muscles here. Not the kind bought and paid for with an expensive gym membership.

This has me wondering what else he's capable of, what other hidden strengths lay beneath his tough exterior. It's a thought process that sees me transfixed when my call is eventually answered.

"Sydney's Glass. We'll help your pane."

I take a second to comprehend her greeting, soon giggling in response.

"Hi there, any chance you can fix a couple of windows tonight?"

While she's initially confident that the company can help, when I give her the measurements that Josh calls out, she changes tack. "I'd love to help. Unfortunately, I'll need to special order something that big."

She pauses briefly, before adding, "It might also be better if you go for toughened glass while you're about it. Much safer."

Blast it, this isn't what I wanted to hear, both from a timing point of view, and my suspicion that 'toughened' will equal horrendously expensive. I'm already feeling deflated thanks to the damage caused by those little brats. I'll not give them the opportunity to cause more. Not if I can help it.

"No, no, I understand. What time can you send someone over tomorrow?"

"Hang on a sec, I'll just check the schedule."

While she does that, I wave to get Josh's attention, with me then tilting the phone away from my mouth. "You may as well get going. This could take some time."

However, he doesn't leave, instead hoisting himself up on the one remaining counter.

I'm busy admiring his muscled thighs when the receptionist comes back to me.

"I can be there at eight for a proper measure up and we can talk about your options. Would that work?"

There's no keeping my response where it is. "You?" After this, I've got nothing. While there's no reason to stop a woman from fixing windows, it's taken me by surprise.

Her resultant laughter tells me I'm not the first person to react this way, either. The booking confirmed, I end the call.

"They can't get here until the morning. Meantime, I'll head home and grab an airbed and some other stuff."

Josh slides down from the counter. "You can't stay here on your own."

After dropping my phone into my purse, I grab my keys, ready to lock up. I then look at him in confusion. "Why not?"

"Because those little jerks might come back. That's why."

He then stares me down, a flicker of something showing in his dark brown eyes.

"Well, yes, I know that, Josh. That's why I'm staying overnight. I'll pick up the loudest air horn available at the gas station on my way back. That'll scare the heck out of those imps if they try anything."

Experience tells me that if the little gang we'd chased up the road are anything like my brother and his buddies, they'll definitely be back.

While spending the night here wouldn't be my first choice, it's better than arriving in the morning to find the place a smoldering pile thanks to illicit smoking.

Next to me, Josh nods slowly as he contemplates my rough-and-ready plan. "Actually, that's not a bad idea. I've got one of those at home, somewhere."

Then, without waiting for me to lock up, he heads for his truck, calling, "I'll see you back here in an hour," over his shoulder.

Without giving me a chance to agree to this, he climbs in, starts the engine and roars off, leaving me open-mouthed, my keys forgotten in my hand.

JOSH

I'm halfway home before I give thought to my actually spending the night with Daisy Green. Of course, with airbeds and air horns in the mix, it'll be anything but romantic. More's the pity, because damn, that woman does it for me.

More than any woman in a long time. And while she's obviously strong and independent, there's also a softer side to her. Like when she stopped Ethan from smashing my Grannie's desk. Even after all these years, I'd still been surprised at how special the memories were.

As I turn into the driveway at my place, I've pushed my memories aside, instead giving thought to what I'll pack for the night. This has me wondering where the heck I'd last seen that air horn.

After opening the door to my garage and standing in front of the wall-to-wall shelves across the back, I undertake a cursory glance. I hope the air horn will jump out at me, but no such luck.

It's definitely been a while since I last saw it. My spotting it without a thorough search was always going to be a long shot.

Thanks to the label and horn both being red, I'm stuck having to check every label on every shelf one word at a time. Sometimes my colorblindness can be a pain in the ass. Stitch that, most of the time, it's a pain in the ass.

And thus, it proves true, with it after five, before I find the air horn in the 'right in front of me' section. It hadn't helped that the horn attachment was taped to the back of the can.

Damn it, now I'm going to have to rush to find all the other stuff I need. Top of the list is an airbed, with me having more than a few to choose from. This was thanks to my forgetting to pack one on more occasions that I'd care to admit.

I've grabbed a single, when I have second thoughts, sliding it back in the cupboard with my other camping gear. A moment's hesitation and I grab a double, because you just never knew.

It's when I grab two sleeping bags I know zip together that I give up kidding myself as to my objectives. I then rationalize my decisions by convincing myself it's because it can get cold at night this time of year.

Lucky for me, I find everything else where I'd expected to, tossing the lot in the back of my truck before heading back to The Daisy Chain.

While there's no official signage up yet, it's how Daisy refers to it, and if it's good enough for her, it's good enough for me.

On arrival at the shop, I'm not altogether surprised to see Daisy hasn't yet returned. In my experience, women treat packing as a marathon rather than a sprint, and as time ticks by, it would appear Daisy is no different.

I'd call her to see if she hasn't changed her mind, but the only paperwork with her number on it is on the counter inside the shop.

Then something catches my eye, and I'm instantly alert. A little head has just popped around the corner of the building, immediately disappearing. A moment later, the process is repeated, although it's a different kid.

This time, the kid doesn't immediately disappear, giving me time to point at my eye and then at them. I have to open the door of my truck for the second kid to retreat. Those little *&%$s, I'd seen the sort of damage kids could cause.

Not on my watch, they're not. Rather than shut the door, I climb out and lock it. No way am I looking for those kids and leaving my stuff at their mercy if they decide to split up.

To catch a brat, you've got to think like a brat, and I've had plenty of experience at that. It's only on reaching the narrow gap beside the shop that I realize I'll never fit down there. The kids jeer at me when they realize I can't get to them.

Damn it, where the hell is Daisy? I've no sooner thought this than she arrives, the back of her yellow 4x4 chock full. Hah, and just like all other women, it would appear she also over packs, with her not needing anywhere near that much stuff to last her overnight.

When she opens up the back of the 4x4, I step in. "Can I grab the key to the front door? We've got company." I follow this up by tipping my head toward the shop, with her soon catching on.

Daisy stares up at me, her eyes slitted, and her mouth a harsh line. "Those little delinquents?"

I nod before taking the keys off her and marching over to the double front doors. I'm inside a second later, wasting no time in sneaking through to the kitchen. Lucky for me, the key is in the narrow gap above the back door where it was always kept.

Even better is when I'm able to unlock the door quietly. I'm just as sneaky when I inch my way out into the trash heap of a backyard.

A quick look around the corner of the building and I spot the kids hunkered down around a makeshift fire pit. It's one that has the potential to spread to the surrounding trash, and then the building.

A deep breath and I explode out of my cover, bellowing at the kids. Their response is immediate, with marshmallows and cigarettes dropped all around. One kid even looks as if he'll have to go home and change his underpants.

"You lot, get the hell out of here. I'm moving in. This is my place now!" After beating my pecs for emphasis, I then add, "If I see any of you here again, there'll be trouble!"

Of course, my threat is empty. But, delivered as loudly as it has been and me doing my best to have the veins on my neck standing out, I doubt they've noticed.

The speed with which they leave says they've taken me at my word and I can't help but indulge in an evil grin. For sure, being confronted by someone like me when I was up to no good as a kid would have scared the crap out of me, too.

I'm kicking dirt into the fire to extinguish it when Daisy joins me, her eyes wide as she takes in the awfulness of it all. Then she smiles, and it's as if the sun has come out.

"What a magical space." She spins on the spot, looking up at the large oak tree that dominates the space. She slowly takes everything in before once again facing me. "Oh, it's going to be wonderful."

I take a moment to put two and two together. "Wait, this is the first time you've been out here?"

She nods emphatically, before adding, "No-one could find the key. I'd added locksmith to my list, but hadn't gotten around to it." She frowns, before walking over and back inside. Sure enough, she soon returns, holding up the old-style key I'd used. "But how did you?"

It was time to come clean with Daisy about the special memories this place has for me. There are also some secrets it holds that she, as the new owner, needs to be aware of.

FIVE

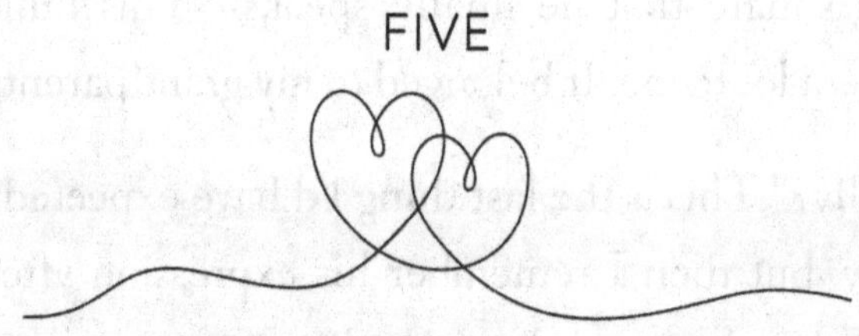

DAISY

Back inside, after Josh had finished extinguishing the fire, I wait for him to speak. It's obvious he's got something to get off that gorgeous chest of his.

Is it wrong that I'm itching to touch it to see if it's as hard as it looks? This has me wondering how he'd react if I did so. Badly, I suspect, with this enough to have me stuffing my hands in the pockets of my jeans.

Not that I can stifle my reaction to him altogether.

Unaware I'm undressing him with my eyes, Josh runs his hand over the peeling wallpaper in the dimly lit dining nook, eventually pulling a strip free. However, it's not until he's concertina folded the piece into a small square that he finally speaks. "This building means a lot to me. It belonged to my grandparents."

"Really?" This is the last thing I'd have expected him to say, but then I remember his expression after I'd told Ethan he was to leave the little office untouched. I'd thought it strange, but now it makes sense.

"Yep, I spent practically every day here after school, doing my homework, or helping my grandpa." He quiets for a moment. "Even the occasional weekend when mom, dad, and my brother were at games."

I'm about to ask him why he hadn't been part of this, but the bleak expression in his eyes has me stopping. Whatever the reason, Josh had been hurt by it, even if him not being involved made no sense.

He had the body of an outside linebacker with a mouthwatering combination of size and speed. Whether him not taking part was by choice or design, I don't know.

The one thing I am sure of is that the town's miscreants are intent on damaging something that holds precious memories for him. And that boils my blood. Even putting my flower shop to one side, I won't let those little jerks ruin the place.

So much of the town's history has already been introduced to the wrecking ball in the name of progress. The thought of the same happening to this lovely old building is enough to have me looking at the kitchen and dining nook in a new light.

Who in their right mind had thought it was a good idea to divide it up with those awful partition walls? It's so much nicer with them gone, even if there's a way to go before it's as gorgeous as it looks in my imagination.

"Alright then. Where shall we set up camp?"

Josh looks around, scanning the cracked windows and graffiti-covered walls. Soon enough, he's once more looking at me, with my body firing up in response and me jamming my hands even further into my pockets.

"I reckon after we've had dinner that we sleep in my Grannie's office. It'll be warmer in there than out here, and definitely warmer than the shop."

After several trips to and from our vehicles, the kitchen and attached nook have a lived-in look about them. Next, I tackle the little office. There wasn't a chance I was putting my airbed, sheets, and blankets on the floor. I hadn't bothered sweeping it out earlier, but then I hadn't planned on lying on the floor at that point, either.

This has me back in the shop where I grab the broom that I'd used to sweep up the glass earlier. A couple of bangs against the end of the counter, and I'm reasonably confident there's no glass hiding in the bristles.

After I've got the little office as tidy as I can, I check on Josh, who's in the hallway with everything we'll need to make a cozy nest. At least I hope it's cozy, because the temperature has plummeted.

Cold air sneaks through gaps around the windows, under doors, and even between floorboards. It was this last that had Josh spreading a ground sheet out, hoping to protect us from the worst of it. We truly are camping out.

Once everything is laid out on the groundsheet, Josh gets to work inflating the airbeds using a foot pump he'd grabbed from his bottomless backpack. While mine is a skinny single that he inflates in no time at all, Josh's airbed is in another league.

We're talking double, snuggle league, with my cheeks warming in response to my vivid imagination. "Do you think they'll come back?"

I really hope they don't, because I like the idea of spending an uninterrupted night with Josh, even if there isn't a chance it'll go as I'd like it to.

But, hey, a girl can dream, can't she?

"I damned well hope not." Josh finishes pumping up his airbed before pressing the stopper into place. "We can't let the little shi... We can't let them get away with any more destruction."

As we work together to make the room as comfortable as possible, I marvel that the building means as much to Josh as it does to me. It doesn't matter that it's for completely different reasons. We're united in wanting to defend it from those awful kids.

We've finished setting up what I now think of as our bedroom and are back in the kitchen, when I suggest we get Door Dash. Josh, however, has other ideas. "Nah, we're good. Let's see what I can rustle up."

I'm wondering what he's talking about when he pulls a small camp stove and pot from his backpack, setting it up on the scarred kitchen counter. He hasn't gotten any further, when the lamp in the dusty light fitting high overhead flickers briefly and then dies.

Yet again, Josh comes to the rescue by unearthing a lantern from his backpack, which, when lit, casts eerie shadows on the walls. He's so much more organized than I am. Once again able to see what he's doing, he then grabs some pouches from the cooler at his feet.

For a start, I think it's army rations, but this isn't the case at all. Rather, we're having beef stroganoff with noodles for dinner.

There's something about watching Josh work that's captivating. Even though he's just putting together a simple meal, he's the first man who's ever done so for me, and I love how he approaches it. There's a quiet confidence I find incredibly attractive.

Once dinner is ready, we eat together, standing at the kitchen counter. While the food might have had its genesis in a large factory, it still tastes delicious, and I enjoy every bite.

"Thank you," I tell Josh as I put my plate in the rusty sink, ready to rinse it off. "That was fantastic."

As he slurps up his last noodle, his eyes twinkle in the low light. He then chuckles, his deep voice filling the room. "Hey, I've got hidden talents."

His expression when he looks at me, has me wondering exactly what those might be. I'm still wondering after we've cleaned up the dinner mess and settled in for the night.

As we lay side-by-side in the dark of the small office, there's something intimate, and oddly comforting, about sharing this strange adventure with Josh.

Rather than turn off the single light in the shop, we've left it going. There's no point when our plan is to deter the kids, rather than trap them. If they know we're in here, then they're more likely to give up and go home.

"I can't believe I'm doing this." My voice, while barely a whisper, is still loud to my ears. "I never imagined I'd buy a rundown building and then have to camp out in it."

He chuckles softly, the sound warming me as it has no right to. "Life's full of surprises, Daisy. But I have to say, you've got guts."

Suddenly, we're interrupted by the sound of voices outside. I tense up and my heart pounds. It has to be the same kids back again, with them sounding even louder and more aggressive than before.

Josh reaches out and grips my hand in the dark, his voice low but firm. "Daisy, it sounds like they mean business. We can't let them destroy this place. You need to stay here."

Hah, it's as if he doesn't know me at all. Then I realize he doesn't. This has me busy kicking free of my makeshift bed, and hot on his heels when he sneaks through to the kitchen.

JOSH

We watch the kids through the filthy window at the back of the building, pleased the light had blown earlier. If not for that, we'd have had trouble watching them without their knowledge.

There's no doubt they're determined to vandalize the building, their faces contorted with malice, visible thanks to the weak outside light. It would also appear they don't care what it takes, nor do they care we might be inside somewhere.

Next to me, Daisy's eyes blaze with a mixture of anger and fear. It's in that moment I realize how much I admire her strength and determination. She's not one to back down, and neither am I.

Our shared determination to protect the building is creating a bond between us, with a growing attraction and undeniable chemistry, at least on my part.

"Who would've thought we'd make such a good team?" I whisper, a smile tugging at the corners of my mouth.

Daisy grins back at me, her eyes sparkling. "Yeah, who would've thought a florist and a construction worker could team up to fight off delinquents?"

Our camaraderie dulls when we watch the kids concentrating their efforts on building a pile of trash next to the back door. It's when I see the tallest boy desperately trying to light a match that I realize the stakes have gotten higher, perhaps even deadly.

"Daisy, you need to listen to me." To keep my words low, my mouth is close to her ear, with me having to fight the desire to kiss her senseless. "You need to get out the front and call the cops. Those little assholes are about to torch the place."

"But I can't leave you. I can help you put the fire out." While I admire her bravery, it's misplaced. The way she holds herself, her unwavering dedication to this place—it's downright inspiring.

"You've got more guts than any woman I know." My voice is filled with genuine admiration. "But Daisy, you need to go call the cops. Things are about to get dangerous."

Eventually, she nods, her eyes filled with determination. "We can't let them win. As soon as I've called the cops and the fire department, I'll be back."

With Daisy on her way to safety, I'm able to relax somewhat. This doesn't last beyond a loud crash reverberating through the room, causing me to jump and let out an involuntary cuss.

Whatever those little assholes just hit the back door with, it was heavy. They must be planning to smash it in to help the fire spread.

"Get away from the effing door!" While I've done my best to sound intimidating, I've mostly been drowned out by the cacophony of destruction outside. The kids' laughter only grows louder, their taunts more vicious as they continue to vandalize the building.

"You think we care what you say?" one of them yells back, emboldened by the support of his friends. "You said this place was yours, but you were wrong, old man!" The kid's tone drips with disdain. "It's ours now, and there's nothing you can do about it!"

And the kid's got the right of it, even if he's still struggling to get a match to light. Not that I'm not capable, but that I'd rather avoid the fallout of my going outside and beating the crap out of them.

Of course, that's not the only option open to me. It's something that once again has me rummaging through my backpack, getting more desperate as the minutes pass.

Eventually, I find what I'm after, my hand closing around the aerosol. Let's see how hard they fight after I deafen them.

A second later and I'm turning the key in the lock, determined to deal to the little shit who's doing his best to smash in the back door. I take him by surprise when I wrench it open and hold the can aloft.

I want it as far away from my ears as I can get it when I press the nozzle.

Only there's no sound. Rather, I've sent a jet of bear spray high into the air with it floating down and enveloping them. The only thing that saves them from being badly hurt by my mistake is them wearing hoodies and masks.

When the spray drifts back in my direction, I don't think twice, slamming the door shut. Despite my quick reflexes, I still get hit with enough of it to have me coughing and spluttering. The irony that I've done more damage to myself than those kids isn't lost on me.

However, when I take the time to listen, I'm also met with quiet out the back. They haven't stuck around, which is a good thing, because the less the cops know about this, the better.

I'm standing looking through the window at the carnage outside when Daisy joins me. "Are you okay?"

She wraps her arms around me in a comforting embrace, with us leaning against each other in solidarity. Tonight could have ended more badly than it has.

I nod, swallowing the lump in my throat. "It's just that I thought ... I honestly thought it was the air horn. I'd never..."

"Shhh, shhh, shhh, I know you wouldn't." Daisy follows this up by stroking the back of my hand, the gesture going a long way toward slowing my heartbeat.

Not until we've left it long enough for the sea breeze to dissipate any traces of bear spray, do I reopen the back door.

As we survey the wreckage left in the kids' wake, Daisy clings to me. My heart pounds as I take in the destruction, the light from my camping lantern revealing all. The kids had gone too far this time, and there's no doubt in my mind that they won't stop unless someone forces them to.

If not for the ringleader having damp matches, the building would be ablaze by now.

"Josh," Daisy says hesitantly, her voice tinged with determination and sadness. "The police and fire brigade should be here soon. Those kids need to learn they can't risk people's lives like that."

"You're right. It could have ended badly tonight."

It nearly had for that one kid. Given my own issues around eyesight, I'd never be able to forgive myself if I blinded him, even if by accident.

The fire brigade arrives before the cops, with us letting them know they can stand down. The cops arrive soon after, with me only just having stuffed the bear spray right at the bottom of my backpack. With none of the kids being harmed, there seems little point in mentioning my mistake.

There are no niceties from either officer. Instead, the shorter one spears Daisy with a look that even has me feeling guilty.

"Are you Ms. Green, the owner?"

Daisy nods wildly before she's able to stutter out, "Yes."

"Can you show us the damage and tell us what happened?"

As we lead them through to the back of the building, all while recounting the night's events, the officers' expressions grow increasingly grim. They take photographs and jot down notes, promising to do everything in their power to track down the kids responsible.

"Darn kids, we never know what they'll get up to next," the shorter officer says as they prepare to leave. "We'll be in touch if there are any updates."

"Thank you." While less than impressed by their lack of enthusiasm, relief washes over me that neither of them detected the lingering scent of bear spray, because I sure as hell can. I'd rather they thought I'd been crying over the damage than because I'd hit myself with that spray.

After watching the cops drive away, I take Daisy's hand and squeeze it reassuringly, before leading her back inside. "We did the right thing. I know it was tough, but this sort of thing can escalate."

"Wow, I don't think I'd like to see that," she murmurs, looking toward the narrow gap in the back fence where the kids had vanished earlier.

I can't shake the feeling that this isn't over—that their vow to seek revenge will only lead to more conflict and tension in the days to come. But for now, at least, we've taken the first step toward protecting what matters to both of us.

SIX

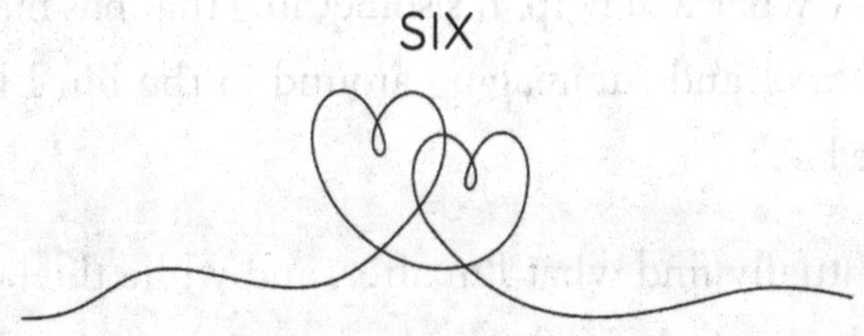

DAISY

Only once I know the kids won't be returning does relief wash over me. We can finally let our guard down, or at least attempt to.

Even after the weight of constant vigilance slowly lifts, relaxation isn't easily achieved in this worn-out building, with chaos still reverberating through the walls.

While the battle is over, Josh seems to think the war has just begun.

"Daisy, I've seen this sort of thing in the past. That ringleader, he'll be pissed I bear sprayed him."

And while that might be true, at least for now, we need to unwind. After closing my eyes briefly, I know exactly what will help. It's something that has me out at my 4x4 and rummaging around in the bin I keep in the back.

I eventually find what I'm after, and while the bottle of red wine isn't the finest vintage, it promises a brief respite from the realities of the night. We've certainly earned a drink. Liquid solace to calm our racing hearts and hopefully lull us into a blissful sleep.

I return to the kitchen, ready to present the bottle to Josh, but he's nowhere in sight, although I soon find him.

He's outside dismantling the pile of trash the kids had stacked up against the side of the building. If that'd gone up, it wouldn't have mattered how quickly the fire department arrived. It would have been all over for the old Victorian.

Neither is he content with simply pushing the pile over, rather he scatters it far and wide, making it that much harder for the kids to reassemble their pyre. The harder we make it for them, the less likely they are to succeed.

Not until he's happy the trash has been strewn to his satisfaction does Josh rejoin me. This has me presenting the bottle to him as a reward of sorts, the label slightly worn from its time being tossed about in my SUV.

While glasses are nowhere to be found, Josh soon unearths a couple of battered stacking cups from his backpack. I guess this shouldn't surprise me, considering what else he's found in there.

The wine is metallic with sour top notes, a taste that mirrors the challenges we've faced tonight, and that still lingers. As warmth spreads through my body, it acts as a salve, soothing the jagged edges of my frayed nerves.

Unfortunately, the warmth of the wine isn't enough to offset the cool of the night, especially after having the back door open while the cops were here. After double checking all the locks, we once again retire to the small office, wine in hand, although we don't bother settling down just yet.

Rather, we sit in companionable silence and sip our wine, the light cast by Josh's lantern giving the small room an intimate glow. Better this than having the harsh overhead light on.

It's not until we've finished the bottle and I'm beyond relaxed and well on my way to tipsy that Josh speaks again.

"Hey, I want to show you my favorite part of this place."

There's no missing the flicker of mischief in his eyes, with mine flaring in response. Intrigued, I tilt my head, a playful smile begging to be released.

"Favorite part? In this decrepit building?" While I might love my new building, I'm not blind to her faults. "Okay, count me in. Lead the way."

Anticipation dancing in his eyes, Josh jumps to his feet and grabs the lantern. He then reaches out with his free hand and, after intertwining his fingers with mine, helps me to my feet.

It's cold out in the hallway, by comparison, something that has me shivering.

"Hang tight. It's warmer where we're going."

Together, we climb the creaking stairs, his lantern piercing the thick veil of darkness. Even in the daylight, the stairwell is dark. At night, without

Josh's lantern lighting our way, it'd be downright creepy.

My heart flutters, alive with the anticipation of what awaits us upstairs. Okay, and Josh's large warm hand enveloping mine doesn't go astray, either.

Upon reaching the landing, Josh leads me down the hallway, its faded wallpaper peeling like memories of the past. The creaks and moans of the old floorboards echo the rhythm of my racing heart.

And then, after rounding the last corner of the hallway, we face a dead end. This was something that had confused me the moment I saw it. And while I'd made a note to check it out further, with everything that had been happening, I hadn't gotten around to it.

After dropping my hand, Josh turns to face me, the narrow space having us just as close as I've been imagining. "Can you hold the lantern up? I'll need both hands for what comes next."

I'm not really concentrating when he passes it to me, my mind full of what he could need both hands for, although I've got a few ideas. Unfortunately, I doubt any of them are on his list.

It's his gentle laughter that has me looking up at him, where there is no missing the glint in his eyes. It's not one I've seen in recent years, and it'd definitely been missing on my date with the book nerd. Surely, I'm reading it all wrong?

Josh, reaching out and running his thumb across my bottom lip, says I'm not. Then I realize that while having more in common with vinegar, this was the wine talking or stroking. I'd be a fool to read it any other way.

After telling me to hold the lantern overhead so he can see what he's doing, a mischievous smile plays on his lips. Lips that soon claim mine in a kiss that nearly has me losing my grip on the lantern.

O.M.G., he kisses how he looks. Firm, and with depth, a combination that floods my body with longing and warms me more than the wine ever could.

It's also familiar, as if I've kissed this man before, as if he's kissed me. The sense of coming home is overwhelming in its intensity. And yet, hadn't it been this way from when I'd first met him? It was as if I knew him, even if there wasn't a chance that I'd forget him.

Okay, now I know it's the wine talking. I need to get a grip before I make a complete fool of myself.

Despite my every atom being focused on both this and our kiss, there's no missing the loud click in the confined space. The "Bingo!" that Josh mumbles against my lips, leaves me unsure if this is because he's unlocked my heart, or some hidden door.

I suspect it might just be both.

JOSH

My lips still tingling from a kiss that nearly had me on my knees, I fumble to open the narrow pocket door as I hadn't in the past.

When I was a kid, I could have activated the hidden lever with my eyes closed. Easy, when I was the one who'd designed it. Well, me and grandpa. He'd said if it was okay for my brother's bedroom to resemble a sporting hall of fame, it was okay for me to have somewhere of my own.

After climbing the claustrophobic staircase, we step into the attic space that spans the back of the building. I hold the lantern high, illuminating the underside of the roof as it soars cathedral-like above us, and a soft gasp escapes my lips. Rather than be empty like the shop and all the rooms below us, up here it's as it was on the day that I'd collected my most treasured possessions.

Just as I was the last person to be up here, it would appear I'm the first to return, and I couldn't be happier with the company. "This always was special to me."

As we walk the length of the space hand-in-hand, I see that even my collection of model planes, cars, and rockets is still proudly displayed, albeit covered in dust. For a moment I'm confused why they're still here, then I remember. At thirteen, I'd said I was too old for them, telling Grandpa he could trash them.

The other thing I'd told him he could trash was my old football. I don't waste time in kicking this out of our way. As if to further taunt me, rather than roll it flip-flops awkwardly thanks to the kitchen knife I'd used to gut it, still being buried deep.

If Daisy's seen my sleight of foot, she doesn't comment.

I'm even thinking I've gotten away with it when she asks, "What's it like? What do you see? You know, color."

For a moment, I'm thrown. How do I explain to someone who sees the world in a vibrant splash of color as she apparently does?

As if unable to stand my silence anymore, she further adds, "Do you see any color at all?"

Despite her clarification, I'm still having trouble coming up with the right words. Where do I even begin?

"I do, but they're faded, you know? They all kinda blend. Especially red."

Instead of commenting, she remains quiet, even if her gaze drifts toward the gutted football still peeping out from under the bookcase.

After a shuddered breath, I grit out, "I'm red-green colorblind, so red looks like a dirty olive to me."

I don't need to say anything more, with Daisy soon enough proving there's more to her than a pretty face and a body that won't quit.

"You went to Coogan High, didn't you?"

I nod slowly, my power of speech momentarily out of action.

The briefest tip of her head toward the dead football, and she carries on. "The team you played that day? It was Freemont High from Taylor's Mistake, wasn't it?"

Again, I nod before huffing out in anguish. Even after all these years, if I allow the memories in, the pain is as fresh as if the game was yesterday.

"I could hardly tell the difference between our guys and theirs. And especially not with a game as fast and furious as that had been. If not for my screw up, we'd have won the game."

As with the memories, my frustration at no longer being able to take part in a game I'd cherished is painfully fresh.

As if picking up on this, she briefly squeezes my hand before refocusing on my old models. As I examine them with her, I'm so very pleased Grandpa didn't get rid of them.

If I ever have kids, I like the idea of passing them onto a son. The same goes for the photos and drawings that adorn the walls, with these a mix of mine and Grandpa's.

"All yours?" Daisy looks up at me, her expression sad, although I'm not sure why. This is a shrine to my forgotten childhood, not hers, although technically, I guess everything belongs to her now.

I nod briefly, my throat constricted with memories of my time up here as a kid. This has me remembering something else. If my grandparents left everything else up here, then surely...

Only once she's put the small rocket she'd been examining back on the shelf, do I lead her to the far end of the attic. Once there, I turn on an antique lamp, surprised when it flares into life.

This sees the area bathed in a warm yellow light, with Daisy's eyes widening further as she takes in the small home cinema.

"I can't believe you've got a movie theater up here," she exclaims.

"Not mine. It's yours now, along with everything else." I gesture as if to take in the entire space. "And it's a brilliant spot to watch a movie."

It's the very act of saying this that has me remembering something else. "Stay here for a second." There's nothing I can do to stop my huge grin. That's if I can pull it off. While the antique lamp had fired up okay, the same might not be true of the other lights.

Back at the other end of the space, I soon discover the old wind-up phonograph under a heavy sheet. It's the same with the ancient records that belonged to Grannie. After making my selection, I wind the ancient beast up and then, as carefully as my shaking hands will allow, drop the needle onto the slightly warped record.

Music from a bygone era fills the attic, with Daisy laughing in delight and making her way toward me.

She's not yet reached me when I bend down and flick a switch, although I'm not confident the icicle lights I'd nailed up as a kid would still work. Everyone knew that if one lamp blew, the rest went out in sympathy.

However, much to my amazement, the attic comes alive with white twinkling lights, further adding to its magical air.

After putting the lamp next to the top of the stairs, Daisy walks to the center of the large space. Then, with her arms out to the side, she slowly turns, her eyes wide, her head thrown back. "Oh, wow, Josh, this is amazing!"

I have to agree, although I'm no longer aware of the lights or the music. It doesn't matter that I've known this gorgeous woman for what amounts to hours. There's a connection that's as familiar as anything from my forgotten childhood.

A couple more winds of the phonograph and I join her in the center of the room, my arms soon wrapped around her in a cloak of desire.

The intimate setting and my longing to bury myself in her, have me drawing her closer with each passing step, with her perfectly in sync. When she stares up at me, her eyes have a languid quality that draws me in further.

I'd be a fool to resist what she's offering and that I've wanted from the first moment I saw her. Why a woman whose whole life is all about color would be interested in a monochromatic lump like me, I'm unsure.

Driven by a hunger I can no longer deny, I reach up, my fingertips brushing against the soft strands of Daisy's hair. The touch sends a thrilling shiver down my spine, a surge of electricity that ignites a fire deep within me.

It's a simple gesture, a subtle invitation, but it speaks volumes of the unspoken connection that exists between us. It's a connection that had been there the moment I saw her atop that rickety ladder.

When the record ends, we're both unsteady on our feet. This doesn't improve when I lead her to the old bed I'd used when staying over. After removing the coverlet and tossing it to one side, we sink into its softness, the timeworn mattress cradling us as we cradle each other.

However, what starts out as a tentative exploration of each other soon fires up, leaving us breathless and wanting more. So much more. In this intimate space, a magnetic pull draws us closer, erasing the boundaries that separate us.

"Daisy, I want you so bad. I've wanted you from the first moment I saw you."

She pulls back, so she can look at me properly, her eyes wide with surprise. "You have?"

I'm nodding in response when she adds, "I thought it was only me."

After her slaying any metaphorical dragons I'd faced, I claim her lips in a kiss that leaves us both breathless. Our tongues tangle as our bodies hadn't when we'd danced. Closer, tighter and so much wetter.

In our desire to be even closer, we desperately tug at each other's clothing until there's nothing between us but the heat of desire. Each touch, each caress, is laden with pent-up passion and unspoken longing.

After making quick work of her messy bun, I run my hands through her hair, glorying in the silky tresses, the scent of her shampoo as perfect as she is.

I'm worried I'm taking things too quickly, when she wraps her hand around my erection, and squeezes tight. She's got quite the grip, and I love it. I also have to wonder if she'll grip me as tightly when I sink into her welcoming depths.

And while that can't come quickly enough, I want tonight to be special for Daisy. I want her to remember tonight for reasons other than those feral kids. This has me breaking our kiss, my lips moving down her body.

There isn't an inch of her I ignore, sucking on her nipples until they're puckered knots of longing, before moving on. Her nether curls are easily as glorious as those I'd tangled with earlier. Again, I take delight in burying my fingers in them, her body twisting in response.

With her most intimate of places spread wide before me, I take delight in swiping my tongue across the little bud nestled there, with her jerking in response. On my continuing to lick it into submission, her moans of pleasure fill the attic.

But I'm not done with her yet. I want her to crumble not just under my lips, but around my cock, with it getting harder by the second. She's teetering on the brink, and I know if I don't bury myself in her silken depths soon, I'll go insane.

The air is filled with the scent of sweat and sex, our heavy breathing almost deafening, when I hear her urgent plea. "Please Josh, please."

She arches her hips, leaving me in no doubt what she wants. It's what we both want, and something I'm soon acting on. After flopping next to her on the bed, I run my hand down her body before burying my fingers deep inside her, stretching her, making her wet.

Not content with simply lying there, Daisy once again takes hold of my cock, with it jumping in response to her gentle touch. As she strokes it, my heart races with excitement and my breath hitches.

This, in tandem with her luscious body being bathed in the glow of the icicle lights, has me close to the edge.

"Careful, Daisy. I'm hanging on by a thread." My voice is barely audible over the sound of our ragged breathing.

After rolling onto her side to face me, she hooks her leg over my hip, giving me even better access to her body. Her silky skin against mine is electrifying, and I can't help but let out a low moan.

"Then, Josh Kendrick, what are you waiting for?" she whispers, her eyes sparkling with desire.

SEVEN

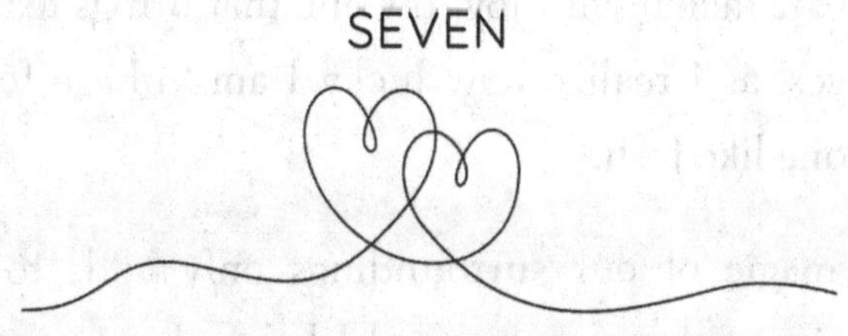

DAISY

Josh listens to my encouragement with enthusiasm, with him pressing me into the softness of the bed. Rather than smother, his weight provides a warm strength that sends me into a frenzy of desire. His breathing is deep and rhythmic, like waves crashing against the shore.

When he enters me, the heat of his skin against mine sends a jolt of electricity throughout my body. Unable to help myself, I arch my back as he slowly drives his impressive cock inside me. Over and over, the friction created by his girth making me moan with pleasure.

He fills me like no man before, and not just physically. There's an emotional connection that has my heart racing with joy. It's one that brings tears to my eyes, as I realize how lucky I am to have found someone like Josh.

The magic of our surroundings only adds to the intensity of the moment, and I know this incredible experience with Josh is one I'll never forget.

In tandem with the icicle lights, moonlight filters through the dusty windows, casting a soft, ethereal glow upon our entwined bodies. As we find sanctuary within each other, the pressure builds so slowly that I hardly notice it at first until I can ignore it no longer.

Every nerve ending in my body is desperate for release. Then Josh sets me free, my cries reaching the very apex of the roof, and unlocking the part of me I've hidden from all others.

A moment later and his shouts of release join mine, his bass notes rumbling through my very core. I've never felt so wanton, or so free, in all my life. Colors are brighter, even the smell of the past that permeates this secret space of Josh's tucked under the eaves is sweeter.

Most beautiful of all, is the man laying hard up against my side, the planes of his body in sharp contrast to my softer form. And while I don't know what the future holds, I wouldn't have missed tonight for the world.

The following morning, I wake, delighted to find my legs splayed wide and him ready for action. I'll take this over an alarm clock any day.

And take it I do, when he glides inside me, burying himself to the hilt, my core rippling in response. I doubt I could ever tire of this, of him.

The only problem is he's not as deep as I'd like. After last night, I know that I'm happiest when it's as if his cock touches my heart. A couple of moves the likes of which you won't see in any yoga class, and I've got him right where I want him.

Deep, so deep.

Although he satisfies me physically, there's still a yearning for something deeper from him. As we move together in the throes of passion, his heartbeat quickens and his breath comes in ragged gasps, our moans filling the surrounding air.

With each twist and turn of our bodies, I'm aware of every inch of him, and yet I feel as though he's still holding some part of himself back. Despite him having provided a glimpse of a world void of color, I feel as though there's more to come, a lot more.

Despite this, we're soon moving in perfect sync, thrust for thrust, the tattoos that cover his chest and arms swirling in concert.

The tension builds with every plunge, to the point I shatter, my body no longer under my control. Josh soon follows me over the edge, collapsing atop me and pressing me into the bed.

And I don't mind, one bit, his solid weight leaving me feeling protected and cared for, rather than squished. I'd be happy to stay like this forever, and we would have, except for us, hearing banging downstairs.

"Josh, did you shut the panel at the bottom of the stairs?"

While he doesn't answer, the speed with which he's moved says, this might not be the case. The thought of Ethan, or any of the other Lucky Break team, finding us as we currently are, and I'm soon moving just as fast.

There's nothing practiced about how we dress, throwing clothes on as fast as we can. Only after he's replaced the dusty cover on the bed does Josh disappear down the stairs. Even from up here, I'm able to hear his sigh of relief, responding with a matching one of my own.

While it's great that he'd shut the panel after us last night, we're not free yet. It's too early to share what we have with the team. I also suspect Josh wants to keep this part of the building to himself. As I take one last look around the space, I realize I want the same, considering this to be our special place.

In our favor is that like a lot of Victorians, this part of the building had been ignored completely. It was clear none of the owners after Josh's grandparents had ventured up here.

Now to work out how on earth we can leave the hidden space without looking as though we've been up to no good. It's a thought that has me hastily stuffing my hair back up in my standard messy bun. The less I look as though I've just been thoroughly bedded, the better.

It's only when we reach the first floor that we realize why we've encountered no one. Everyone is out on the sidewalk, looking at the building, shock marring their handsome features.

On joining them, Josh and me, soon sport similar expressions. How on earth had we missed those little brats doing this? And then I remember exactly why, with my face coloring as flashes of last night flicker to life.

The only plus is that rather than take my blush as one of embarrassment, Ethan interprets it as anger. And, to a certain extent, he's not wrong. I can't believe the damage caused by those delinquents, with it far worse than I'd have thought possible.

They're only kids, and yet this is the sort of damage I'd expect an adult to inflict. And we're no longer talking about a couple of broken windows. The threats painted on the walls, and the missing siding, amount to thousands of dollars' worth of destruction.

"Damn them. I'll have to get the cops back. I'll need their report for the insurance claim."

Ethan swings in my direction, a worried frown already in place. "Get them back?"

· · ·

With the glazier put off until things are more settled, and work on hold until the cops have been and gone, we assemble in the kitchen. Thanks to my having packed my machine, we're enjoying fresh coffee when Josh and I recount the events of the night before. Well, not all of them, obviously.

Cole Stillman is the first to react to Josh's story about the kids piling trash against the back of the building.

"Arson? That's serious."

And so is Cole when he says this. Seriously, there's something scary about this guy, although he's only ever been nice to me. Despite him being older than the others on the team, I get that he's more than capable of keeping up with them.

Josh puts his empty mug in the sink before responding. "Yeah, and potentially lethal with Daisy and me inside."

He's no sooner said this than there are knowing looks all around, and I color again. So much for us sneaking around earlier. It's as if the team is psychic where their workmate's love lives are concerned.

Which is ironic, given I don't even know where Josh and I stand as regards a relationship.

"I can't sit idly by and watch these kids destroy my livelihood. I won't let them win." While my assertion had started out as a distraction, a desire to protect what's mine soon courses through me. If I can gather evidence and present it to the authorities, they'll have to take action, won't they?

The cops last night hadn't exactly been optimistic about finding the kids responsible. It had been more a case of them going through the motions than displaying any intention of catching the culprits. If they won't take action, then I'll make sure they have no choice.

Rather than looking specifically at Ethan, who appears supremely pissed about something, I look to the rest of the team. "Do any of you know anything about setting up security cameras?"

If I can capture the delinquents in the act, I can pass it to the authorities. And if they don't take it any further, then the footage will mysteriously appear on various community Facebook groups. Someone has to know who these kids are?

While not my first choice, the damage done to the front of the building said it was only a matter of time before someone got hurt, or worse. The final straw had been seeing the scorch marks on the front of the building.

If the boards that covered the windows had caught alight, they'd currently be identifying Josh and me thanks to our dental records.

The team don't even need to speak for me to know Malakai can help with setting up surveillance, with all eyes on him. Never, when I purchased this building, could I have foreseen anything like this.

I'd expected that in a month's time, the renovations would have been completed and that I'd have The Daisy Chain up and running again.

As it is, I'm now fighting for the very survival of the building, with that impacting my solvency. The last thing I need is to be making mortgage payments on a building that's not yet renovated, or worse, been damaged beyond repair.

However, as the team springs into action, with Malakai heading straight off to pick up some 'equipment', my pessimism is replaced by optimism. Add in all the stolen moments with Josh, and there's definitely a spring in my step by the end of the day.

JOSH

That night, there isn't a chance Daisy and I can enjoy a repeat performance. Not with half a dozen men crowding the space, and the air thick with the smell of sweat and anticipation.

While the plan is to catch the kids in the act, we don't want to risk any further damage to the building while we're about it. Once we've got the footage that we're after, we'll be all over the little devils like ham on rye.

After dinner, the team moves through to the shop, taking a hodgepodge of camp chairs with us. Daisy puts hers next to mine, our hands gently clasped in the dark.

Everyone is focused on the screens hooked up to the cameras without being visible from the outside.

Daisy tipping her head toward me, has me doing the same, meaning I'm the only one to hear her whispered words over the murmur of the guys chatting.

"Josh, what if we don't catch them? I can't afford to keep paying the mortgage with no money coming in."

There's tension in her voice, as though she's being choked by her financial worries, and all I want to do is make them go away. I wanted to tell her that everything was going to be alright, but I didn't know if it was true.

All I could do was sit with her in the darkness, hoping for the best.

The sooner we catch those little assholes in the act, the sooner we can get on with the renovation. We don't have to wait long, with Malakai's gasp having me look in his direction. A moment later and he's holding the screen up to show what's happening outside.

"Sheesh, is that a blowtorch?" Cole is on his feet with impressive speed for an older guy, and soon enough is armed with a wooden baseball bat. He's quietly unlocking the front door when he stops and turns to Malakai. "Mal, it might be an idea if you turned the recording off for that camera."

Whilst Cole's words have been quiet, there's no missing their weight. Things are about to get serious, making me happy he's on our side and extremely capable.

Despite this, I surge to my feet, energy pulsing through my body as I ready myself to follow Cole outside. However, my excitement is short-lived when Daisy's small hand wraps tightly around mine, halting my movement.

Her breathing is ragged, and there's tension in her grip as she holds my hand. The responsibility of protecting her weighs heavily on my shoulders as I realize that if I step outside, Daisy will follow me.

Her wild nature may be endearing, but it also puts her in danger. This realization causes a knot to form in my stomach, and I know that keeping her safe is my top priority.

This sees us watching the screen with Malakai, while Cole and the others confront the arsonist. Cole stabs the baseball bat in the kid's direction, but rather than being cowed, the kid does his best to set fire to the bat.

Cole's not having it, with him swinging it, although the kid isn't his target. Instead, he sends the blowtorch out into the street, where it lands in a shower of sparks.

Disarmed, the kid doesn't wait around to see what happens next, with his speed impressive. Neither Cole nor any of the others take off in pursuit, although I would have. I already know I can outrun that little jerk.

I doubt he's as brave without his blowtorch.

It's Daemon who walks out onto the road and grabs the blowtorch. He's careful how he holds it, though, even using a pair of pliers to turn it off.

It wasn't until he brought the torch back inside and we turned on the overhead light that we noticed something. This isn't any old cheap model available pretty much anywhere. This is trade quality, and hardly something you'd expect some snot-nosed kid to be armed with.

Of more concern is that it's got the *PROPERTY OF LUCKY BREAK CONSTRUCTION* engraved on the side.

And while I know Coogan's Break is small, it's not that small. For this torch to be used to set fire to a building we're currently working on, is too tidy, by far.

I then have to wonder if this is payback for the bear spray incident?

For sure, that kid had been pissed when I took him out, even if I copped more of the spray than he did. However, my gut is telling me there's more to this than pure coincidence. A lot more.

I also have to wonder what would have happened if we hadn't caught the kid at it? Would the blowtorch have conveniently been found amid the charred wreckage of the building?

It's highly likely we'd be confronted with charges of negligence, even if we weren't found guilty of arson. Cole seems to share the same opinion as me, and I can tell I'm on the right track because if anyone knew about shady behavior, it's this guy.

A moment later, and Cole has his phone out and is calling Ethan. Rather than indulge in chitchat, he gets straight down to it. "Do you remember when you had all that gear stolen?"

Given he then walks through to the kitchen, the rest of the conversation is lost to us. Add in Cole's tendency to keep things to himself, and the chances are that we won't hear what else he and our boss have discussed.

The next morning's meeting at the local police department is friendlier than I've been expecting. In my experience, providing cops with evidence they should have sorted themselves never goes down well.

I'm sure that would have been the case if we were dealing with those from a couple of nights back. However, with Detective Johnson and Officer Ramirez a step above, we're welcomed into a room that's filled with the aroma of freshly brewed coffee.

While the Detective smiles at Daisy and me when he hands us our coffees, he only gives Cole a cautious nod.

Damn, but I'd love to know what that guy's story is.

Once we're all settled, Detective Johnson stares at each of us before speaking directly to Daisy. "Thank you for coming down, Ms. Green." He pauses for a sip of coffee and perhaps to center his thoughts. "We've reviewed the footage, and unfortunately, we think we know the culprit."

Apart from him using the word 'unfortunately', there's no missing the resignation on the guy's face, at knowing who's responsible. Given how confrontational the kid had been with Cole last night, the little asshole has to have had run-ins with the law in the past.

And if that's the case, why do the cops appear reluctant to follow this up? I've come to no conclusions when Daisy speaks.

"I don't want to lay charges, Detective. A strong warning will suffice."

On her other side, Cole turns to look at her, his surprise clear. "I don't know if that's a good idea. I've seen his sort in the past. Whatever the hell set him off, he won't back down easily."

However, this isn't what captures Daisy and my attention, with us turning to look at the detective. Despite him having muttered to himself, there was no missing his, "You got that right!"

Daisy huffs out, before speaking again. "My building, my choice. And anyway, the only thing he damaged was those old boards covering the windows."

Both the detective and officer look relieved at this turn of events, although it's the senior of the two who responds. "I think that's the best course, Ms. Green. Once we find him, we'll put the fear of God in him."

I haven't even finished my coffee when everyone else gets to their feet, with the meeting apparently over. This has me draining my mug in a single long draft before joining them.

My hand on Daisy's back, I steer her gently out the door. Even this brief contact is enough to have a tingle of excitement from my fingertips to other parts of me not on show. A hitch in Daisy's breathing says, I'm not alone.

However, I'm not ready to leave just yet. "Detective, you'll tell us when you've spoken to the little... young man, won't you?"

Next to me, Cole nods his support of this. "Until then, we'll keep him in line."

There's no missing the thinly veiled threat in Cole's words and the detective sucking air into his lungs. I'm expecting him to speak, but he says nothing.

EIGHT

DAISY

Half-an-hour after our return from the police department and I'm still out front of the building. Next to me, Cole and Josh are engaged in a heated discussion about the next steps.

As they talk, I'm only half-listening, my thoughts preoccupied by the Detective's words from earlier. Eventually, I can keep quiet no longer. "Guys, shouldn't we leave it to the police to sort out?"

Cole's response to this suggestion is fervent. "Miss Green, we can't just rely on them. We need to scare the crap outta that little jerk. That kid needs to understand that actions have consequences."

As if to highlight what these might have been, he runs his finger through the scorched patch on the boards protecting the front windows. He then continues, leaving a trail of soot behind.

"We need to take a stand and make it known that we won't put up with any of that crap. We need to strengthen security, if nothing else."

Before I can give my full consent, he's already heading inside, leaving me with Josh. "He's right, Daisy. The police can't be here all the time. We have to take matters into our own hands if we want to protect your place."

His conviction surprises me, and I can't help but wonder what has stirred such intensity in him. As I reach out to touch his arm, trying to offer some reassurance, I realize how close we've become in that moment.

With Cole inside, Josh slings his arm around my shoulders, drawing me closer. "Don't worry, sweetheart. We'll install more security cameras, motion sensors, and arrange for increased police patrols. We'll also throw up some signs to warn that little ratbag about the consequences."

His voice resonates with genuine concern and there's no missing his deep connection to the building. I can't help but be touched by his dedication to safeguarding what I now think of as *our* project.

"That's a fantastic plan, Josh." I squeeze his hand on my shoulder. "Let's get to work on it."

The rest of the Lucky Break team agrees with this rough-and-ready plan. All going well, we'll only need to make it clear to our little vandal that we're not putting up with any further destruction. While there might have been other kids also hanging around, he's definitely the ringleader.

Once we've got through to him, they'll move onto easier pickings. At least this is the hope. One thing that I'm definitely pleased about is that I've put a hold on the replacement glass for the front windows.

Too tempting by far, and I doubt the insurance company would be happy with me if I had to hit them up for yet more glass. It'd also do awful things to my premiums, something I can't afford at present.

With the plan confirmed, our focus returns to the renovation of the shop, now with a heightened sense of vigilance. To address my concerns about safety after dark, I propose that at least two people should always be on-site overnight.

"As the building's owner, I'll, of course, be one of those people."

Even though the men initially resist my idea, after some negotiation, a compromise is reached. Two men will be on site with me, and one of them will invariably be Josh.

He readily agrees to this, perhaps too readily. "I'll bring more supplies from home after work. That way, we won't need as many trips back and forth."

Encouraged by his response, I'm quick to join in. "Sounds good to me. I'll do the same." As I notice the curious glances of the surrounding men, I realize that our enthusiasm might have been a bit too clear. I chide myself for not tempering my reaction, especially where Josh is concerned.

With the men engrossed in security upgrades, construction, and shelving for the shop, I set out to visit neighboring businesses. I'm determined to uncover whether anyone else is being targeted by the same delinquents.

To my dismay, it turns out that all the businesses in the area have suffered to varying degrees, with it mostly petty vandalism. Despite this, it's disheartening to see the extent of the damage inflicted on the community.

It's also disheartening that none of the other business owners want anything to do with catching the kids responsible. Their preference is to keep their heads down rather than draw attention.

Back at The Daisy Chain, I join the men for lunch, enjoying the comradery, with me mostly having lunch alone in my old shop. My friend Skye rarely got away in the middle of the day. She was too busy keeping her bakery customers happy, with lunchtime one of the busiest for her.

As I cast furtive glances around the team, I decide I enjoy having company. A peek at Josh, and I decide I'd like a lot more than that.

After the men have gone back to work, I look out the open back door at the debris crowding the yard behind the shop. It could be so beautiful out here, especially in summer, with the canopy of the large oak providing ample shade.

It would also be the perfect spot for me to have outdoor plants and garden furniture. All of it for sale, of course. There were definitely times of year when the floral side of my business died off.

If I could balance this out with other sales, then so much the better. And seeing as I had the space, I may as well make the most of it.

On hearing movement out in the hallway, I turn to see Josh coming back to fill up his water bottle.

"Josh, how easy would it be to knock down the back fence?"

His brow wrinkles before he answers me. "Depends. Do you want to put it back up again? If you don't, then we can attach a chain to the back of one of our trucks and rip it out in a heartbeat." He tips his head to the side, letting me know he's not finished. "I guess the question is why?"

I step through the back door and out into the yard, as far as the trash will allow, before turning to face him. "I was thinking I'd like to clean this lot up." At least this was something I could do on my own, and it would also cut down on things those kids could burn. "Could we get a dumpster back here?"

He joins me, his gaze drawn to the fence as if to see how it's been constructed. After a bit of head scratching, he nods slowly. "I'll ask Ethan if I can get started on that this afternoon, and get him to book a mini dumpster."

He then has another look at the sheer volume of trash that surrounds us. "Better make that a big one. You'll also need some proper gloves, because who knows what crap is buried out here? Last thing you need is to be scratched by a needle, or whatever."

Until he'd said it, the thought hadn't even occurred to me, but he's right. Just because Coogan's Break is a bit of a backwater when compared to the likes of Los Angeles, drugs are still about.

JOSH

As the day progresses, I make quick work of dismantling enough of the fence to allow a dumpster to be dropped into the backyard. While I complete this, Daisy works hard on tidying a space big enough to take it.

And damn if she isn't a sight to behold. The only thing wound tighter than some of the rusty screws in the fence is my cock.

It's been back-breaking work, with us ending the day, filthy and tired.

As we stand shoulder to shoulder surveying the fruits of our labors, she shuts her eyes, a beautiful smile playing around her plump lips. "Oh Josh, it'll be wonderful by the time we've finished."

"Good lord, woman, but that's some imagination you've got there."

When I look at it, all I see are sepia-toned piles of trash awaiting the dumpster. Obviously not what's in her mind's eye.

I realize having the backyard tidy will be a great addition to her shop. It'll also be somewhere she can relax when she's not working. I've only just finished thinking this when she points at the far back corner.

"And that's where I'll put the hot tub." She follows this up by stretching tall, and then twisting first in one direction, then the other. There's no missing that she's as stiff as I currently am, although a hot soak wouldn't help me.

As tempted as I am to work some of her kinks out, I instead pat her on the shoulder, with her turning to face me. "I've got something I need to sort inside. I'll catch up with you soon."

"Okay, I just want to finish tidying up a little more." And with that, she picks up the rake and continues corralling the carpet of leaves over to the corner that will one day house the hot tub.

I could definitely benefit from a hot soak right now, and all going well, I'll soon be doing just that. Everyone but Malakai, having left for the day, it's eerily quiet inside.

I'm at the bottom of the steps when I spot him through the front doors of the shop. He's on a stepladder, busy installing another camera.

Instead of heading upstairs, I join him out front. "Is that the last of them?"

He nods rather than speaks, his mouth sprouting the screws required to fasten the camera.

"Okay, I'm just heading upstairs. Are you okay to lock up here when Daisy is inside?"

Again, he nods in response, and with Malakai being one of the most reliable individuals I know, I'm happy leaving him to take care of this. Meanwhile, I need to finish up my special project.

I'm almost back at the stairs when I hear the unmistakable sound of him spitting the rest of the screws into the palm of his hand. What he says next has me grinning.

It also has me taking the stairs two-at-a-time, all the while whistling to myself, with my evening having just got a lot better. Daisy won't believe what I've got in store for her. I'm on the landing before I smell roses.

Great, this means the water has heated enough to form steam. Hopefully, it's not too hot, because I need a soak, and soon. Lucky for me is that the temperature is perfect. Hot enough to make me hiss after I drop my clothes in an untidy pile and climb in.

But also, not so cool that the water will be lukewarm before I've had time to enjoy myself. Time to enjoy Daisy, who I hear plodding up the stairs.

Sure enough, when I listen carefully, I hear her arrive on the landing, then I hear her sniffing. She continues this as she walks the length of the hallway. Her expression when she opens the door and sees me luxuriating in the bubble bath is priceless.

The air, being thick with steam, gives this a dream-like quality which works perfectly. I've been dreaming of this moment since filling the bath just after lunch and setting up the immersion heater.

Daisy wastes no time, shutting the door and sliding the bolt to lock us in. She's just as quick to strip, taking as much care of her filthy clothes as I had with my own.

When she sinks into the water with a hiss and leans back against my chest, my arms automatically wrap around her. Only when I squeeze tight and she groans do I realize she's feeling the manual labor more than I am.

This has me changing tack. Much as I want to seduce her to the point we empty the tub with our shenanigans, I instead work on her sore muscles.

"I hope Malakai has a lot more cameras to install."

I chuckle at Daisy's heartfelt observation, feeling the rumble of this as surely as she is. The peace that rolls over me when she settles even more doesn't last long.

Having her this close, and naked, has thoughts of last night rushing back. Of how well we fit together, of how she made me feel.

And I'm not just talking physically here, either. I wouldn't be human if I could ignore that. No, there's something about this gorgeous woman that gets to me, in a big way.

After years of keeping people at arm's length, I've allowed her to get closer than anyone else. Hell, I'd even opened up to her about my colorblindness last night, and that never happens. Well, not this early in a relationship.

Relationship? I'm not so sure about that, but we've definitely got something if I'm prepared to lay myself bare, like I did.

Too many times in the past, revealing my one weakness led to people teasing me, and with college football, downright deriding me. Even the guys on the Lucky Break team rib me about it from time-to-time. And while I laugh along with them, I don't find it funny.

Daisy further relaxes against my chest, the hair escaping her scrunchie tickling my nose. "Oh, I needed this, Josh. There isn't a spot that doesn't hurt."

She takes a deep breath of the rose-scented air before continuing. "How on earth did you get the water hot? Didn't Ethan say the water heater was an accident waiting to happen?"

Busy massaging away any knots I come across, I'm slow to answer in my determination to have her as relaxed as she'd been last night. "He did, but because the tub is cast iron, I could get the water hot using an immersion heater."

She exhales again, her hands coming to rest on my thighs where they're wrapped around either side of her. Damn, we're lucky the bath is the size it is, with neither of us shrimps. While it'd been a pain heating all that water, the extra room is now benefiting us.

When her fingers glide up the inside of my thighs, my heart races with excitement, my breathing ratcheting up in response to her touch. Every nerve ending in my body is alive with anticipation, my cock throbbing with the promise of pleasure.

Daisy's head drops back, her form languid. "It's just a shame we can't take our time."

My burst of laughter in response to her despondency echoes off the walls of the spartan room. "You'd be dead wrong about that, beautiful."

As I continue massaging everywhere, that's tense, and even a few places that aren't, I explain why we can take our time. Sure, the guys might give me grief about my colorblindness, but there are pluses to your teammates knowing you well.

It was for this reason Malakai had picked up that I wanted some time alone with Daisy that evening. Despite the guy's taciturn nature, he doesn't miss much. Something to do with his past, I suspect, although what that was, who knew?

Like a lot of the guys on the team, he keeps his past in the past.

Either way, he'd announced out of the blue that he had plans for dinner. Plans he hadn't mentioned up to that point. That he'd be gone as soon as he'd installed the final camera. Something that should have happened by now.

"So we can take our time in the bath. Well, at least until the water cools." I follow this up by rubbing a sudsy sponge over her breasts, with her back arching in response.

By the time I've finished with her, she's squeaky clean and I'm feeling really dirty. It's a good thing I'd been organized between bouts of carefully dismantling the back fence.

Because of this, Daisy's bag is tucked behind the door, and I've also got a clean change of clothes. There wasn't a chance either of us could get back into the ones lying in a heap next to the bath.

They're almost as filthy as my thoughts, even if these will have to wait. After drying off and throwing on my clean clothes, I leave Daisy to finish dressing. Before things get any hotter, I want to make sure Malakai has left for his hastily arranged dinner.

Sure enough, I find his freestanding tent set up in the shop, with all the doors locked, and a note from him on the counter.

Back at 8. I'll take it through to midnight. M

A glance at my watch lets me know Daisy and I have two hours before he's due back. And when that happens, she'll need to be up in the attic rather than bunking down in the small office, even if that's where Malakai thinks she is.

I then laugh to myself. With how that guy's mind works, he probably knew about Daisy and me before I did.

The other thing that's a given is that he'll be as regimented with patrolling the property as he is with everything else. I'll just need to wait until he's outside.

Only then will I be free to sneak upstairs and join her, even if part of me realizes the sneaking isn't really necessary. Still, it might be better if Daisy doesn't know that with her as likely to want to stay downstairs to preserve her reputation.

But to hell with rolling around on the floor with that gorgeous woman when there's a perfectly good bed at the top of the house. The trick will be to keep that spot a secret, because I doubt even Malakai knows about it.

Around quarter-to-twelve, I can nip downstairs, and be in the small office ready for him to wake me up to take over.

NINE

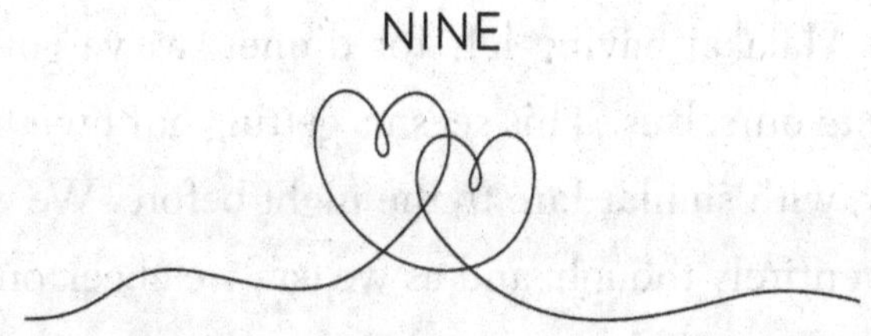

DAISY

Freshly dressed after our bath, I join Josh in the shop and there's nothing I can do to stop my burst of laughter. For sure, there hadn't been a bright orange tent filling the space when I was in here earlier.

Josh slings his arm around my shoulders before answering my unspoken question. "I know it's weird, but Malakai will be warmer bedding down in that, out of any drafts."

As if to back-up his words, the wind makes its presence known by whistling through any gaps in the boards covering the front windows. Despite Malakai and Josh nailing them tightly together, there's no keeping Mother Nature out when she wants in.

With Malakai having left for dinner, we've got the place to ourselves. This sees us getting our own meal ready, with similar fare to the night before. We can't relax entirely though, and as we eat, we check on the bank of small monitors connected to the various cameras.

Eventually, I spot something that has me leaning forward for a closer look.

"How on earth did he get a camera down that side of the building?" I follow this up by tapping the screen so Josh will know which one I'm talking about.

On him peering at it, I can see when he gets my drift. That space is only fit for a child, something he knows from experience, our little vandal having used the confines to his benefit.

For a security camera to be covering the narrow space, must have made for some clever maneuvering on Malakai's part. And it wasn't as if the guy was a lightweight, his body definitely not designed with gymnastics in mind.

There's nothing I can do to stop the thought of Stripper Gram, but with real muscles, from flashing in neon in my brain. It's something I share with Josh through my giggles.

He's still shaking his head when he tells me about the roster for that night. Just as Malakai is a whizz installing cameras, it was him who'd said a 4-hour rotation would be the best balance between being alert and getting enough rest.

It's a timetable that will see me in bed before eight, although you won't hear me complaining tonight. Not when I know Josh will join me as soon as he can.

On Malakai's return at eight, I've been in bed in the attic for ten-minutes. Apart from when Josh tucked me in, the evening had been strangely quiet. The only things picked up by the cameras were a couple of rats and a lone raccoon. He was such a little cutie with his wee burglar mask.

Josh wasn't as enamored. Telling me Trash Pandas—raccoons—could be a nightmare. He'd even made me promise not to encourage the little devil. Not only was it illegal to have them as pets in California, but they can cause even more trouble than rats.

His face had been awash with disbelief when he'd added, "It's as if they think wearing a mask somehow makes them impervious to danger."

And if what he says about them getting into trouble is right, we'll definitely have to put a board in the dumpster when it arrives in the morning. Much easier if they can find their own way out after they inevitably fall in.

It's only five-past-eight when Josh sneaks up the stairs to the attic. But rather than join me in bed as I've expected, he stands by the window, peering through a gap in the blanket we'd nailed up there earlier.

In concert with looking down into the backyard, he checks his watch now and then. Intent as he is, I don't pepper him with questions, knowing I'll hear soon enough. He maintains this vigil for half-an-hour, before nodding to himself, stripping and joining me in bed.

"What was all that about?"

Josh kisses me on the forehead before answering. "I wanted to make sure of Malakai's circuit, so I know when it's safe to go back downstairs."

This makes sense, because so far as Josh's workmate is concerned, we're spending the night in the small office. Certainly, that's where our air mattresses and sleeping bags are, something we'd made sure the others knew by leaving the door open.

When Josh drags me closer, and his lips lower to mine, for a moment I'm fully into it. "Hang on, hang on. We need to be up and about at midnight. Do you think this is a good idea?"

His expression, visible in the soft illumination from the icicle lights, says that he thinks it's an excellent idea. I start again. "Okay, it's a great idea, but is it a wise one? What happens if we have trouble?"

"Damn it, you're right." He follows this up with a wicked grin. "Three hours' sleep should be plenty." A moment later and he's loosened his hold on me and is shimmying down the bed.

I've no doubt where he's heading, and after last night, there's nothing I can do but open myself to him in silent invitation. We're short on time, damn it. We need to make the most of it.

A moment later, his hot mouth engulfs my jewel, and he slides a couple of fingers deep inside me, wriggling them about to devastating effect. It's all it takes for all thoughts of surveillance to be obliterated, along with any reticence on my part.

Eleven-thirty comes almost as quickly as I just have. So much for getting three hours' sleep. I'm noodle-level-relaxed, which isn't good with a four-hour watch ahead of me.

Josh isn't in much better shape, with him slow to climb out of bed and get dressed. When I try to do the same, he pushes me back down. "And what do you think you're doing?"

"What do you mean? I'm getting up to take the next watch."

Josh shakes his head. "Like hell you are. You get some sleep."

I'm struggling to get past him when he leans down. "If you behave yourself and stay in bed, I'll have a treat for you when I finish my watch."

There's no missing the promise in his eyes, the sensual light enough to have me subsiding. He then gently rolls one nipple, and then the other, with me squeaking, although not in alarm.

When he follows this up by repeating the motion with my clit, my reaction is more of a whimper, full of need and raw desire. There's some consolation in him looking as loath to leave as I am for him to do so.

There wasn't an inch of me he'd neglected. With each minute, he'd gotten to know my body better through touch and even taste. Hah, especially taste. One swirl of his tongue was enough to have me shaking with need and begging him to fill me with his impressive length.

In return, I now know what drives him crazy. Crazy enough, I'd had to swallow his shouts of release for fear Malakai would hear.

On hearing him close the sliding panel into place one floor below, I fall asleep with a smile on my face and a delicious ache between my legs. What can I say, I asked, and he delivered, big time. Oh, so big.

· · ·

If I thought he'd want to rest when he returned four hours later, I'd be wrong. His breath smelling faintly of coffee tells me he has no intention of sleeping. And after four hours of being in a coma, I'm up for whatever he's got.

And he's got plenty, not wanting to waste time if the haste with which he strips is any indicator. Soon enough, he's whipped the covers back and settled between my thighs.

When he slides inside me, I'm complete, my hips arching to help him drive home. And drive home he does. My heart pounds, as if it might burst with emotion.

The sparkling of the icicle lights only adds to the dreamlike atmosphere of the attic as Josh fills me over and over. My body quivers in response to the point I'm overwhelmed, the climax cutting through me, leaving me fizzing.

I'm not alone though, with Josh's shouts of release muffled when his mouth mashes against mine and we collapse.

His length still filling me, he gently rolls us to the side and envelopes me in a crushing embrace. When he kisses me goodnight, the coffee on his breath mingles with the musky scent of our lovemaking.

His breathing then settles, syncing with my heart, and despite the caffeine buzz he'd admitted to earlier, he falls asleep, his grip on me never loosening.

JOSH

On opening my eyes, I blink owlishly, trying to make sense of where I am. I'd gotten nowhere near enough sleep last night.

Outside, birds chirp in the oak that dominates the backyard, the leaves rustling in the gentle breeze. I stretch my arms and legs, luxuriating in the crispness of the cool sheets against my skin.

Daisy is snuggled up next to me, her hair tickling my nose. The sweet scent of her shampoo and her warm breath against my cheek when I lean over to kiss her make for a peaceful moment. It doesn't last long.

The volume of light sneaking around the edges of the blanket covering the window tells me it's late. Not late-late, just later than I'd like it to be.

A check of my phone sitting on the battered apple crate next to the bed tells me we've got forty-five minutes before the team turns up. A reasonable amount of time, but nowhere near long enough for what I'd had in mind.

Daisy grumbles when I disentangle myself, and as tempting as it is to roll over and carry on where we'd left off, it's not a risk I can take. While Ethan might be more relaxed these days about us getting to know the clients better, he's nowhere near fully on board.

Leaving Daisy tucked up in bed, I tiptoe downstairs. Only after I've stood with my ear pressed against the sliding panel for a couple of minutes, do I inch it quietly to the side.

Out in the hallway, I take as much care when I close it before heading straight for the bathroom. Rather than have the tub as full as yesterday, I fill it enough that Daisy can have a decent rinse off.

The last thing I do before returning to tell her she's got ten minutes before she needs to get up is to rig up the immersion heater. Just because I need a cold shower doesn't mean she can't enjoy a few of life's luxuries.

While Daisy does her best to rouse herself, I make for the kitchen. The last thing I do before sliding the concealed panel shut behind me is to check it's not visible. Nope, unless you were really on the lookout for it, you'd never see it. Exactly as grandpa and I designed it.

That worry eased, and I'm on my way downstairs for a much-needed cup of coffee. I might even need more than one after last night.

But I wouldn't have changed it for the world, even if Malakai gives me a knowing look when he joins me in grabbing a coffee. It was a good thing that Daisy had thought to bring her machine over. Instant wouldn't have been up to keeping me awake this morning.

It's half-an-hour before she makes an appearance, looking delightfully disheveled. That her hair is wet tells me she'd enjoyed the bath I prepared for her. Fixing the water heater is something I make a mental note of, because it's definitely not on the main punch list.

When that was prepared, Daisy hadn't been expecting to move in until after the shop was renovated. The shop had always been her priority, with renovations to the accommodations something of an after-thought. Not any more.

Malakai is first to finish his breakfast of two coffees and a protein bar. "When you two are ready, I've got something to show you." He follows this up by rinsing his coffee cup and putting it on the draining board.

I'm not sure if it's what he's said, or how he's said it, but I'm soon gobbling my pop tarts, with Daisy following suit. Soon enough, we're traipsing through the shop hot on his heels.

I've expected to see something out of place, but it's as it had been last night, except that Malakai's tent has been tidied away. The same is true when he opens the front doors and we follow him out onto the sidewalk.

Other than the scorch marks on the boards covering the front windows, everything was as it had been yesterday. It's only when he looks pointedly up that I spot what's wrong.

"But, but how the hell?" I don't get any further my mind busy thinking back on every second of the night before. Nope, I hadn't seen a damned thing on any of the monitors. Nor had I seen anything when I checked out here during my shift.

"But how come none of the monitors went black? I checked them regularly. They were all fine."

Daisy's gasp lets me know when she also spots the damage. "Oh, Malakai, I'm so sorry. I'll pay for a replacement, of course."

She follows this up with something under her breath. And while I can't hear what she says, her expression speaks volumes. She's pissed, and rightly so. I'm kinda feeling that way, too. The damage happened under my watch. When I catch that kid...

The only one not worried about the damage is Malakai, an evil grin splitting his face. "Catches them every time."

Without explaining further, he pulls his phone out of the back pocket of his jeans. That he's searching for something is obvious. Even more obvious is when he finds what it is he's after, taps the screen and hands the phone to me.

Daisy crowds close to watch the video. It's not from the camera that's been hit with black spray paint, but from a much smaller one mounted above the front doors.

Two things immediately become apparent. The camera vandalized had been a dummy, and that was no kid, but a man. And one stupid enough to pull his mask down after taking out what he thought was the only camera.

When I look back at Malakai, he's no longer smiling. "You know him from somewhere?"

Malakai nods briefly before huffing out. "Don't let the guy's beard fool you. You know him, too."

Daisy's gaze swivels back and forth between us, with her obviously unsure who she should focus on. "Who? Who is it?"

I have to look at the footage three more times, and even take a screen shot before I see what Malakai is seeing. "Rod Baker? But didn't he leave town after Ethan fired him?"

Malakai tips his head in acknowledgement, confirming everything I've said.

"But if we have a name, can't we go to the police?" This question from Daisy has both Malakai and I looking at her, although I'm the one who answers.

"Yeah, it's not quite that easy, Daze."

I've not decided how to break the news that Ethan won't want to report it to the cops when he arrives, immediately picking up not all is well. After Malakai shows him the camera footage, he's furious.

Especially so when he grasps that this might be why a blowtorch with Lucky Break Construction etched on it had been used in the attempted arson.

However, it's Cole who points out the obvious when he's shown the footage after his arrival on site.

"That little sh...," He stops, looking at Daisy. "That little delinquent. You don't suppose he could be Rod's kid, do you?"

Some rough-and-ready calculations and it's agreed that he must be and that it makes more sense than coincidence. The kid's old enough, for sure, with it doubtless a case of like father, like son.

The only thing we're in the dark about is why Rod would target Ethan after all this time. If indeed Lucky Break Construction is the target.

It's something that has me turning to Daisy and taking her hands in mine without thinking. "Daisy, what did the other businesses say about the attacks on their premises?"

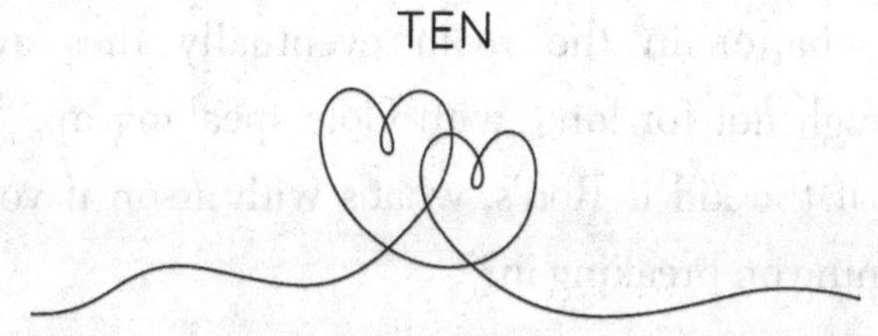

TEN

DAISY

The Lucky Break crew don't start work immediately. Rather, they sit around in the shop on any flat surface they can find. I listen intently to Ethan, learning that Rod Baker had been caught stealing from a previous construction site.

Ethan had taken pity on him and given him another chance, but the guy couldn't resist the temptation to steal again. It had been too much for Ethan, who'd fired the man on the spot.

"I couldn't risk word getting around that my team was dodgy. Not with so many of them trying to get back on their feet." Ethan shakes his head in disbelief at the past being back to haunt him.

The chatter in the room eventually dies away, although not for long, with Cole speaking up. "But even if the kid is Rod's, what's with arson if you're planning on breaking in?"

He's raised a good point. There's no sense in burning my place to the ground if you want to steal any tools left on site.

"What if they're not?" I know they've heard my half-formed thought because of the way they're all staring at me. "What if they're not working together, that is? That the kid isn't related to this Rod guy?"

They don't climb all over themselves to agree with me, with even Josh looking skeptical.

After shrugging, I say the next thing that comes to mind. "Hey, it's that, or he painted the camera so we wouldn't see him when he torched the place?"

I've barely finished saying this when Cole disappears through to the kitchen and out the back door. Meanwhile, Malakai walks back out the front. However, it's Cole who yells out first.

There's a log jam as everyone tries to enter the small hallway at the same time. Eventually, though, the men step back, allowing me to go first. After walking out the back door, I soon stop in my tracks.

The leaves I'd raked up just the afternoon before were now a smoldering pile with the fence behind them, still glowing in places. How on earth did Josh and Malakai miss this? If not for us having had rain recently, the damage could have been a lot worse.

And if the fence had caught properly, it was close enough to the building that the siding would have soon been ablaze. On looking up and seeing the blanket over the attic window directly overhead, I'm unable to stop from shuddering.

It could all have ended badly, possibly even tragically. Apparently no longer caring what his boss or teammates think, Josh wraps his arms around me and holds me tight. He only loosens his grip when I stop shaking, something that takes longer than it should.

Malakai breaks the silence that had fallen thanks to everyone being deep in thought. "While that bastard might have painted over all my dummy cameras, everything else is still up and running. I'll pitch my tent out here tonight. Someone else can take the shop."

Other members of the team are also quick to volunteer to stay over. As well as protecting the property, they want to see if they can catch Rod Baker. Or his son, if that's who the kid is. Either would be good, both of them even better.

Ethan whistles loudly to get everyone's attention. "You lot take care of that. I'm going to see if I can't track that asshole down." He frowns briefly before continuing. "Someone has to know where he's hanging out."

His expression tells me that if he finds his old employee, it won't end well for the man, and I can't altogether blame him. If I'd given someone a second chance and they'd repaid me like that, I'd be fuming, too.

The only thing the team agrees on is that the guy will be back tonight whether he's out to torch the place or burgle it. Either way, he has to do so in person. And when he shows up, they'll be waiting for him. The only thing we have no way of knowing is whether he'll have his son or apprentice with him.

The guys don't care either way. I get that it's personal, with the men keen to keep their jobs, something that can only happen if Lucky Break remains in business.

Any further discussion is interrupted when the truck with the dumpster arrives, the beeping as it reverses, drowning out the birdsong. That thing is enormous, and yet, as I look around the backyard, I wonder if it might not be big enough.

The stuff in the backyard isn't only down to the businesses that have inhabited the premises, but to others throwing their trash over the fence. As well as the standard stuff you'd expect, there are also old rusted out washing machines, and even a fridge. None of them are in working order.

Soon enough the rental company have craned the dumpster onto the site, setting it down with a loud boom in the spot I'd cleared for it. It's a good thing one end has doors that open halfway up. Without these, I'd be lucky to get anything into the high-sided beast. "Is this the largest size you have?"

While waiting for his workmate to unhook the chains that secure the dumpster, the guy manning the hydraulic controls nods. "Hell no, lady. We got way bigger than this. You want I should change it out."

I can't say NO fast enough. It'll be enough of a challenge as it is, without dealing with something even bigger. As it is, I'll need the help of the Lucky Break team to get the various appliances hefted into the dumpster.

Not a chance my 'can-do' attitude will be enough to deal with those. Instead, I'll be concentrating on getting rid of anything that's flammable. The less fuel-load in the backyard, the safer it will be.

As I pull on the heavy-duty leather gloves Josh had given me, I take a moment to have bad thoughts about the people responsible for the trash. I'm dreading the task until Josh rejoins me, pulling on a sturdy pair of gloves of his own.

Okay, with him at my side, suddenly the task isn't so taxing.

And this is indeed true. The bright sun beams down on us while the chirping of birds and rustling of leaves fill the air. If it wasn't for the threat of arson later that evening, the day would have a celebratory feel to it.

Our morning of hard work pays off, with the area already looking a lot tidier. The only thing that's not tidy is Josh and I. We're filthy thanks to our hard labor, and in no fit state to eat inside.

It's something that sees us having one of the team pass us our camp chairs and lunch. There's no point hosing ourselves down until after we've finished our task, with us enjoying our lunch in the cool shade of the massive oak tree.

As I watch Josh enjoying his sandwich, his disgusting t-shirt in a heap on the ground next to him, I realize I'm looking forward to hosing him down later. In fact, I can hardly wait.

When I share this with him, he bursts out laughing, before telling me he won't be the only one who'll be wet after that happens. The promise in his eye says it all, and I have trouble swallowing my last mouthful of sandwich.

JOSH

Despite wanting to load the dumpster quickly, I force myself to slow down, conscious of Daisy's limitations. I don't want her to feel rushed or overwhelmed. It was also for this reason that I'd had some of the team help me with the big stuff right off the bat.

Far easier that we toss the washing machines and that ancient fridge in the dumpster's bottom than try perching them on top of everything else.

Thanks to the sun now being at full strength, the air is thick with the smell of garbage, my nose wrinkling in disgust. Despite the stench, there's a certain satisfaction as I toss each item into the dumpster.

However, this satisfaction is dampened by the persistent ache in my groin. Daisy's snappy comment earlier about hosing me down still lingers in my mind, the images I'm dredging up not helping my erection in the least.

By the time we finish loading everything into the dumpster late in the afternoon, I'm not only filthy, I want to be even dirtier. At least where Daisy is concerned. When I'd promised she'd be wet by the time I'd finished with her, I'd meant it.

It was payback time for me sporting wood for the better part of the day. Of being on the edge of losing it, and to hell with having an audience.

The plus now is that we're on our own, albeit briefly. But that's okay. It won't take long for me to have her begging me to fill her. With this in mind, I rip my gloves off and toss them on the ground. I'm scooping her up soon after.

She stinks. But that's okay, because so do I. We're a match made in trash heaven. Her squeal of surprise flashes around the backyard, but I don't slow until I set her down next to the hose.

She's still laughing when I turn it on and hose her down. While it's nowhere as nice as luxuriating in the bath, it's more effective. Now and then I'll turn the hose on myself to help with the smell wafting up in waves.

As I make her turn this way and that, the water splashes back at me, droplets hitting my skin. It's when I notice her nipples showing through her t-shirt in response to my swishing the spray back and forth that things get out of hand.

After gasping in surprise, she grabs the hose. Normally, a groin full of cold water would take the edge off my erection, but I'm way past that point now.

Only by gritting my teeth do I remain intact.

"Oooh, I'm sorry. I didn't mean to hurt you."

She's distracted enough that I'm able to regain control of the hose, with me taking delight in grabbing the front of her shorts and shoving the hose down there. Now it's her turn to squirm.

If not for Ethan making an appearance, I'm not sure how things would have ended. As it was, I yanked the hose out of her shorts and set about hosing myself down.

By rights, I should shove the hose down my own shorts, because I'm now so close to blowing, it's not funny. As calm as I'm likely to get, I then turn the hose on the fence, dampening it down, droplets of water glistening in the sun.

Not long after we'd found the smoldering pile of leaves this morning, Malakai had looked over the fence. Sure enough, there on the ground had been a pile of spent matches.

This was why neither he, nor I, had seen anything, with whoever was responsible—presumably Rod Baker—hidden from view by the tall fence. It was for this reason Malakai had scaled the oak tree and installed a small battery-powered camera that linked to an app on his phone.

It's something I remember only when Daisy is talking to Ethan about him not having got a bead on his old employee. Damn it, Malakai will have seen Daisy and me fooling around with that hose. I need to be more careful.

There's nothing quiet about dinner that night. Malakai has been joined by Daemon, Cole, Spencer, Zac, and Tyler. I'm especially grateful for this, with both Zac and Tyler being in established relationships. They hadn't needed to take time away from their families to help, and yet here they were.

Cole was always going to be on board, with him taking a zealous interest in anything underhanded and dodgy. Rather than make do with more camp food, we order in Chinese, although we draw the line at beers.

Given we've got a potential arsonist in the mix, we need to be alert, to deal with anything we might face.

Despite my trying to convince Daisy that she'd be better off moving back to her friend Josie's house, she'd refused.

As we dig into the takeaway meals, the conversation revolves around strategy. Cole, being the oldest and most devious, leads the discussion while everyone else throws in ideas and suggestions.

I'm grateful they're all taking this seriously. Despite being friends for years, we all know that sorting out Rod Baker and that kid is required if we're to keep the Lucky Break name clean.

After finishing the last of the food, we split up. While Cole has set up in the shop, Malakai has pitched a tent in the backyard. It's not the bright orange number he'd spent last night in, with Cole having taken up residence in that.

And why? Because we don't want to give Rod a heads-up that we're on to him. And nothing says lookout like a bright orange tent on display. Tonight, Malakai is sleeping in a tent so camouflaged, you'd trip over it before you saw it.

As for Tyler and Daemon, they're pretending to leave, although they won't be going far. While

Daemon will park his truck up the road and hunker down with binoculars, Tyler has driven to a friend's place around the corner.

That his friend's house also backs onto the alley that runs behind Daisy's property is perfect. He'll be able to keep an eye out that way, without being visible.

Meanwhile, Zac and Spencer are making the most of the makeshift camp in Grannie's office, even using Daisy and my sleeping bags and airbeds. I'm happy about this, wanting her to be as far from any potential action as possible.

However, we won't be in the attic tonight. Remembering the shock on her face when she realized how close the building had been to catching fire, isn't something I'll forget in a hurry.

That's not to say we won't have fun passing the time. It's armed with a strong coffee each that we make our way up to the front room on the second floor.

From here we have a bird's-eye view of all the roads that lead to The Daisy Chain corner. If anyone so much as walks in our direction, we should be able to see them.

We're on for four hours before Zac and Spencer take over. Once they're in place, Daisy and I will do our best to get some shuteye in the small office. I'm not sure our chances of doing so are great.

But I can live with that.

ELEVEN

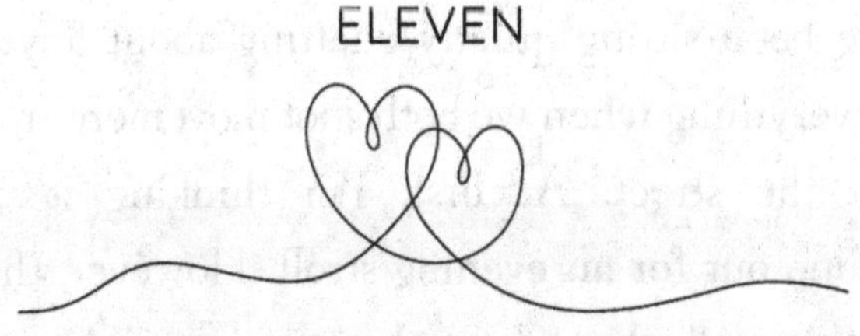

DAISY

Despite carrying our camp chairs up to the front room on the second floor, conditions are low rent. The room isn't even carpeted. Rather, the bare boards are covered with a fine layer of dust that's accumulated over the years.

Tonight couldn't be more different from last night. And yet I'm happy sitting in the dark next to Josh, my hand in his. There's a companionship I've not experienced before.

Unlike Malakai out in the backyard in his tent, or Cole bedded down in the shop, we're able to talk.

Despite this, we keep our voices down., barely above a murmur, and all the more intimate for it.

We've been sitting quietly chatting about anything and everything when we both spot movement further down the street. At first, I'm thinking it's just someone out for an evening stroll. However, there's something off about how the guy is walking, with Josh's aside telling me he's of the same opinion.

It's when the first guy is joined by a kid that we know our suspicions were on the money. Rather than get up, Josh leans to the side and grabs the small radio Malakai had given us before we'd all gone our separate ways.

"Breaker, breaker. The Phoenix is in flight. Little bird in tow."

We get confirmations all round, with everyone holding their positions for now. The idea is to catch the pair, not scare them off. We're still sitting there when I notice two men trailing our quarry.

Ethan. One of them is definitely Ethan Hunter, Josh's boss. I'm not sure who the other guy is. Despite only having met the Lucky Break Team a week ago, I don't think he's one of them. However, the longer I watch him, the more I realize I know him from somewhere. But where?

Josh and I are tucked away on either side of the window when man and boy disappear under the verandah of the shop. On the other side of the road, Ethan and his friend have disappeared into a hedge that fronts a property there.

If I hadn't seen them vanish with my own eyes, I'd have thought I imagined them. Another quick peek and I see Daemon easing his way out of his truck and quietly shutting the door.

It's only now that I realize that we're trapped up here. The stairs make too much noise for us to sneak down, at least not without warning the intruders or, should that be, arsonists?

On my pointing this out to Josh, he immediately grimaces, although not for long. "I don't want you anywhere near this guy. He's like a rat when cornered. And we've already seen what a nasty piece of work that kid can be."

He follows this up by sliding a small headlamp into place, although he doesn't bother turning it on.

Despite his warning that I should stay back, when Josh makes his way out of the room and over to the top of the stairs, I'm tiptoeing behind him. If all hell breaks loose as we're expecting, then staying quiet will no longer be an issue.

And soon enough, this is exactly what happens. Once the shouting starts, Josh turns and grabs me by the shoulders. "Daisy, I want you to stay up here." He follows this up with a resounding kiss that has me rooted to the spot.

After flicking on his headlamp, he's flying down the stairs, taking them three at a time in his haste to be part of the action.

Now, as well as shouting, there's a lot of banging and crashing and a heck of a lot of cussing. Apparently, Rod and that kid aren't going down easily, even if they do eventually, in quite the pile if the sound effects are accurate.

The quiet that follows has me brave enough to inch my way down the stairs, stopping on each tread as if to gauge the wisdom of my actions. I'm near the bottom when Josh yells out for me to come down. His volume is such that I can tell he thought I was still upstairs.

My hand plastered against my chest, I work on settling my heart before stepping down into the hallway and through to the shop. Even with every light switched on and several of the team armed with flashlights or headlamps, nothing could have prepared me for what I saw.

A man, who I have to assume is Rod Baker, and the little vandal from a few nights back, lie bound and gagged on the floor of my shop. Next to them stands the man who'd been with Ethan earlier, with me recognizing him immediately.

"Oh, Chase. Hi." My wave is as weak as my words have been.

It's the first time I've seen my friend Josie's husband next to his brother Ethan, with the resemblance marked. The only thing I don't understand is why we need a bounty hunter here.

If not for Ethan cringing and Chase hitting me with a death stare, I'd not have realized I'd said anything. I'm not sure how I could have forgotten that bounty hunter is a dirty word in the Hunter household.

Heaven knew Josie had warned me about it often enough.

JOSH

With Ethan's brother off delivering Rod Baker to the cops, and the guy from welfare services having collected the kid, everyone else had gone home. Daisy and I now have the place to ourselves, with no risk of interruption.

After locking all the doors, we fly upstairs, making for the attic. I've never stripped as fast in my life, unsure if this is down to the adrenaline of the takedown, or Daisy's proximity.

And I'm not alone in making haste, with Daisy soon just as naked, the icicle lights casting shadows on her gorgeous body, her smile beatific. Two steps are all that's required for me to be hard up against her. So very hard.

Her softness is in stark contrast, and yet there's nothing weak about this luscious woman. She hadn't freaked out when she'd entered the shop earlier and seen our unwanted guests hog-tied.

After the chaos of the preceding days, our world now seems to have come to a standstill, with the air filled with a deafening silence. And while my entire universe now revolves around Daisy, I'm unable to relish the moment.

My heart races and my palms are slick with sweat. "I guess with that sorted, I'll be able to move back to my place tomorrow."

I hold my breath while waiting for her reaction. She has my immediate happiness in her hands, even if she doesn't know it. However, she'll not hear this from me. I want her to choose me for the right reasons, not the wrong.

As I hold her close, she stiffens in my arms; her gaze fixated on my chest. After a while, she slowly raises her head, with the pain etched in her dark blue eyes hitting me hard.

The air is thick with tension when she finally speaks, her words halting. "Is that what you want?"

I try to answer, but the words stick in my throat. I haven't stood up for what I want in so long that it doesn't come easy. And yet, I know, deep down, that I want Daisy. Any how, and for as long as she'll have me.

I start by nodding, then have to clear my throat. "I'd like to stay. If that's okay." Not since I stood in front of my coach at the end of that disastrous game all those years ago have I been this nervous. Actually, I'm way more nervous now.

The pain in her eyes is soon replaced by joy, with this a perfect match to her beaming smile. Next thing I know, she's thrown her arms around my neck and is kissing me, with her passion saying more than words ever could.

Everything that came before this lovemaking pales compared to what we share now. Our coupling is every bit as magical as our surroundings, with her body glowing under the icicle lights.

It's as if we can't get enough of each other, as if neither of us can believe it's real, as though it will end before we've had our fill. I keep waiting for the bubble to burst, which happens sooner than I'd have thought.

However, it's not Daisy who bursts it, but hammering on the sliding panel at the bottom of the hidden staircase.

There's no missing Cole's, "You need to get down here, now!"

I'm alert in seconds, as is Daisy next to me, with both of us scrambling to get to our feet and get dressed. Not once in all the time I've known Cole have I ever heard him speak with this urgency. Even worse, is that he hadn't spoken, he'd yelled, with this enough out of character for the alarm bells to be deafening.

Next to me, Daisy knows nothing of this, with her on edge simply because of the older man's abrupt tone. "What is it? What's wrong?"

Her asking this while we're still making our way down the narrow stairs as quick as is safe, does no good. "I'm not sure. I don't even know why he's back. He said he was going home."

The shop was again as brightly lit as it had been after the team had caught the intruders earlier. The difference is that Cole stands there alone, the shop doors still tightly locked.

"I did my best to catch him, but he was too quick for me."

I'm still processing what he's said when Daisy speaks.

"He escaped?"

Cole apparently catches on quicker than I do. "No. Not him. Some other guy."

Finally, my mind catches up with my thoughts. "A guy? Not a kid?"

Cole tips his head in acknowledgement while passing a tatty piece of paper over to me. However, before I can take hold of it, Daisy grabs it. She's as quick to unfold it and scan the contents.

Despite not knowing what the note says, there's no missing her reaction, with her sinking to the ground, the note fluttering down next to her. Now I'm torn. Do I help her stand, or do I read the contents of the note?

In the end, comforting Daisy wins out, with me dropping next to her and dragging her into my arms. Her sobs cut straight through me. Whatever the hell that note says, it's serious. Certainly, it's way beyond kids mucking about.

Looking over my shoulder, I catch Cole's gaze. "What the hell does it say?"

Cole picks it up, but rather than read it out loud, he holds it so that I can read it myself.

GET OUT!
BAD THINGS WILL HAPPEN
IF YOU STICK AROUND.
REAL BAD THINGS.

After reading it, I'm glad he's done so, because Daisy didn't need to go through that again.

It's rare in our modern world to be threatened like this, and yet that's exactly what's happened to Daisy. When I'd first looked at the letters cut out of a newspaper, my initial reaction had been to laugh.

However, there's nothing laughable about the import of the words. The only thing I don't understand is why. Despite not having known her long, in my heart, I know Daisy is a good woman.

Not the sort to attract venom like that displayed in the awful note. We've not discussed potential motives when Daemon and Tyler return. They're soon followed by Malakai, Zac, and Spencer.

Of Chase, there's no sign with him presumably still filling in paperwork down at the police station.

Only then do we hear that on leaving Cole had sensed he was being watched, a sensation he'd listened to. "Can't tell you the number of times it's saved my ass. Anyway, I left in my truck, parked around the corner and then circled back."

But despite him wasting no time, he'd not returned soon enough to apprehend the guy. "I saw him stuffing something under the door, and I yelled out, but he was off."

Tight up against me, Daisy shivers, reminding me she's had quite the shock. "Come on, let's get you back to bed. We can deal with this in the morning."

A brief nod from Cole, and I know he and the others will keep a watch on the place until then. It's time we took this seriously, because that note says it's not Lucky Break Construction that's the target, but Daisy. Whoever had sent it wants her out of the building, and even gone from Coogan's Break.

I'll do anything to protect her, even if it means putting myself in harm's way. I'll be her shield, her guardian, and her protector if she'll have me. She's a good woman, a nice human being. She deserves nothing but love and happiness, and I'll make sure she gets it.

TWELVE

DAISY

Back in bed with Josh, I stare unseeing at the icicle lights overhead. I'm having trouble coming to terms with the threat in that cobbled together note. It's left me both scared and angry, with the scared part having me even angrier.

I hate backing down, with this part of the reason I've made such a success of my business. "I'll be darned if I'll let some jerk run me out of this building."

Next to me, Josh props himself up on one shoulder. "Hell no, we won't. However, it might not be safe to stay here. Not until we know who we're up against."

Strange, but until he'd said it, I hadn't given thought about who was actually targeting me. I guess it was easier to think of whoever sent the note as a faceless nobody.

Try as I might, I can't think of anyone who'd hate me that much. The only person I've had words with in recent times was my old landlord. I then dismiss him out of hand. He's too lazy to bother cutting out the letters for a note.

No, if it was him, he'd say them to my face, and have fun doing it.

Despite Josh's tender lovemaking, sleep doesn't come easy, and I wake feeling gritty and out of sorts. As my mind crowds with images of last night, my unease only increases.

A cold bath and pop tarts for breakfast doesn't improve my mood. Around me, there's no missing the Lucky Break team is also subdued. While they're continuing with the upgrades to the shop, any sign of banter and whistling is strangely absent.

Part of me is even wondering if there's any point in continuing with the renovation. Another more stubborn part is thinking, "Hell yes, there is."

It's this that has me standing in the shop, ticking items off my list, when there's a knock at the front door. Rather than let me open it, Josh does so, deliberately putting himself between me and our visitor.

Soon enough, though, he stands to one side and I see that it's Maureen Bennett, the realtor who'd sold me the property. She's carrying a small bouquet and a bottle of bubbly, presumably as a moving in gift.

I can't help but notice the bouquet is utilitarian, although I won't quibble, because, to me, fresh flowers are always welcome. We step forward at the same time and she hands the bouquet to me, while Josh grabs the bubbly.

When she makes it obvious that she wants to come in, I step to the side and gesture with my free hand. "Please come through to the kitchen." I then lead the way, with Josh bringing up the rear, although he doesn't stay after putting the wine in the fridge.

Next to me, Maureen looks around, amazement clear in her expression. "You've done so much already." Her words carry the same surprise as her gaze, although I'm not sure why. Did she expect me to buy the building and then sit around doing nothing?

I hold back none of my enthusiasm, even if this has taken a battering after last night's events. "Yes. All going well, I'll be able to open for business in a couple of weeks."

This is a complete guess given the challenges that have been thrown up. I'm not letting her know that, though. If there's one thing that I've learned from being in business, it's that you don't show your hand.

Apparently, Maureen hadn't learned this lesson. "Oh, I was thinking you might have changed your mind. Decided it was all too much." The hopeful edge to her words immediately has me on high alert.

"Heavens no. Once I decide on something, that's it."

Again, I inject false enthusiasm into this, and once more, I'm rewarded with her looking crestfallen. There's something off, although I'm unsure what.

"You were so lucky to get this place. There was interest... He was so angry..." She falls silent, nibbling on her bottom lip, before starting up again. "I don't suppose you'd consider selling?"

My expression must say it all, with her answering her own question.

"No, no. Of course not. Never mind, I'll just let you get on with things."

She's turning to leave when I ask her the question that's been buzzing in my brain ever since she said someone else was interested. "Ah, who was it? Who was after the property?"

Honestly, I doubt I'd have got such a reaction if I'd slapped the woman. Her gaze darts around the kitchen as if looking for an escape. Her first words when she tries to answer are incomprehensible. "Ah, ah, I couldn't, possibly. I'd ..."

Eventually, I take pity on her. I'll get no sense out of her in this state, instead showing her through to the shop and out the front door.

It's not until this has been closed behind her I tell Josh and the others what she'd inadvertently let slip.

Cole and Ethan, who'd arrived while I was with the realtor in the kitchen, talk over each other in their eagerness to speak. The upshot being that if we can determine who'd wanted to buy my place, then we'll know who wants me gone. At least this is the theory.

It's then I remember the response I'd got from the old guy who owns the dry-cleaning shop next door. He'd been nervous when I asked him if he'd been targeted by the neighborhood's delinquents.

"Josh, can you come with me?" I've already opened the front door, making it obvious I'm going out. However, it's been the very act of asking him to accompany me next door that has me realizing how rattled I am courtesy of that note.

Only yesterday, and I wouldn't have thought twice about visiting the dry-cleaners on my own. That's no longer the case, and I hate it, even if I enjoy having Josh along with me.

On walking past the front windows of the shop next door, there's no missing a couple of spots that have obviously been hit with rocks. However, the glass here appears to have been up to the challenge unlike that at my place.

The moment I enter the shop, I'm immediately struck by how bare it is. Not three days ago, the rail that snaked its way through the shop had been weighed down with clothing.

Today only a couple of items remain. The other thing that's missing is the overwhelming scent of dry-cleaning fluid. That strange fresh but chemical aroma that is common to these establishments.

It still lingers, but is nowhere near as strong as it had been when I last visited. I'm still wondering about this when Mr. Brettell, the owner, walks through the doorway behind the counter.

"Ms. Green?"

That's it, that's all he says, and I immediately know something is up. Perhaps it's the apologetic edge to his greeting. The realization of why then hits me like a freight train. "You've sold, haven't you?"

He's still nodding when I continue. "Who to?"

When Josh leans on the counter and eyeballs the poor old man, I almost feel sorry for him. And if it weren't for me needing to know, I'd back down.

Eventually, though, he stutters out, "It's a developer. I can't say who. He made me sign something. If I say anything, he'll sue me." Then, as if feeling he has to justify his decision. "It was a fair offer. As good as I could hope for after, you know ..."

On returning to The Daisy Chain, I'm seething. Not only has some developer bought the old guy's property out from under him, he'd driven the price down first. No wonder my place had been as cheap to buy as it was.

I can't help but snort-laugh as I imagine the developer's face when he'd discovered I'd beaten him to it. Now all I need to do is work out how I can keep hold of it, or at least stop him from burning it to the ground.

JOSH

I don't blame Daisy for being angry about this developer trying to force her to sell. Ethan's just as angry when he hears about it.

"Those assholes. They're ruining this town. Ripping down anything historic and slapping up an ugly concrete box in its place."

The annoying thing is that there's nothing to tie the attempted arson to anyone other than Rod Baker and that kid. For sure, whoever the developer is, they must be paying Ethan's old employee one chunk of change. The guy has apparently remained tight-lipped other than to say Ethan Hunter got everything he deserved.

It was Chase, Ethan's brother, who'd kept us abreast with developments on that front. After helping rid the department of more than a few dirty cops, he had access to information others might not.

Based on Rod Baker's animosity toward Ethan, the developer would've had no trouble convincing the creep to burn The Daisy Chain to the ground. And if what Ethan says about the town's developers is true, the scum behind the attack had probably saved on the hit thanks to Rod's personal vendetta.

Ethan's expression is grim when he grits out. "Cutting corners is the one thing those assholes are good at." He tips his head to the side, his gaze skittering about enough to tell me he's thinking about something, although I don't need to wonder for long. "I'll get Lindsey onto it. If anyone can get the skinny on who's behind it, it's the women in her book club."

Unsure of when he'll ask his wife, and how long the town's biggest gossips will take to get back to him, we're at a standstill. We're all standing around wondering what happens next when there's another knock at the door.

However, there's nothing tentative about it this time. It's then followed up by a woman yelling, "Open the door before I drop this lot!"

Daisy is quick to act. "It's Skye!" On her opening the door, it's hard to see who's out there, the visitor obscured thanks to a teetering pile of bakery boxes. However, I immediately recognize the logo, with me salivating in response.

There's also no missing when others on the team get a whiff of sugar, with them wasting no time in stepping forward and grabbing box after box. These are soon spread out along the counter, their lids flipped open to reveal the tasty treats inside.

While it's apparent that we're eating the rejects, none of us care. A misshapen cupcake still tastes as good. The same goes for all the pies and pastries.

In between stuffing ourselves with enough sugar to have us bouncing off the walls, we discuss how we're supposed to work out which developer it is. We can't simply rely on the ladies in Lindsey's book club. That might take weeks.

It's our visiting pastry chef who comes up with what might be the fastest solution.

"Slap up a FOR-SALE BY OWNER sign and say the price is negotiable. Surely that'll bring whoever's behind it out of the woodwork?"

There's silence as everyone looks at her, momentarily stunned. And yet what she says makes sense.

It's not long before we're all nodding and trying to talk at the same time. It's something that has more than a few flakes of pastry finding their way onto the floor. It's organized chaos, although it's easy to see we're all in agreement.

As much as Daisy is ready to go to Home Depot and buy the biggest sign they have, I put my hand on her arm to slow her. "Hang on. We need to finish up a few things first."

While her confusion is clear, she soon puts this into words. "Like what?"

"Like setting up a make-shift sprinkler system." This from Malakai has everyone looking at him. He shrugs before carrying on. "We need to cover all our bases. Make sure that bastard can't burn the place down."

Ethan adds his support for this. "That makes sense. This guy doesn't care what happens to the building. Chances are that once he buys the place, he'll demo it, anyway."

"But I'm not selling!" Daisy's tone is indignant, a perfect match for her stance.

I rub her back, doing my best to calm her down. "We know that. But he doesn't. Well, he won't until we're ready for him."

Soon enough, we've demolished all but a few of the wonky treats Skye had brought for us, and the woman is ready to leave. "Daisy, are you sure you should stay here? Whoever is behind all this sounds dangerous."

I add my support to this suggestion, with Daisy glaring at me. "I'm not going anywhere. I refuse to have this creep push me out of my own, ah, home."

While I understand where she's coming from, that note haunts me. Sure, the guy was probably only out to scare her into selling, but if he's happy to hire Rod Baker, he's not a nice guy.

The question is, am I willing to risk it just being a nasty scare tactic rather than a promise? Hell no. Not where Daisy is concerned.

I'd never forgive myself if anything happened to her. I just need to convince her to move back to her friend Josie's place. I'll feel a lot happier knowing Ethan's brother, Chase, is on site, too.

As much as I'll miss her company at night, it's a sacrifice I'm prepared to make. I can only hope she's amenable to my suggestion.

I'm about to make it when I hear a familiar beeping. Could this be a case of being saved by the dumpster? And to be honest, I'd had no clue how I was going to talk her into moving out. Perhaps because, deep down, I didn't want her to?

Actually, there was no deep down about it. Despite the challenges we're facing, I'm loving my time with Daisy, both of us out of our usual environments. Neutral ground, if you like.

This then gives me pause. Is it really neutral ground, when I feel more at home in this building than I ever have in the ranch house I'd bought on a whim? Not wanting to face that right this minute, I instead turn to Daisy.

"You want to make sure your little bandit mate isn't in there before they take it away?"

Such is her determination to ensure this doesn't happen, that she's in the backyard ahead of me. There I find her yelling and waving her arms around to get the attention of the guys hooking chains to the corners of the beast.

As if knowing what she wants without her saying so, I walk over and open one door at the back wide. Sure enough, there's a raccoon staring up at me, caught red-handed, the remains of someone's lunch in his paws.

Of more concern is that he, or should that be she, isn't alone, with three cubs also at the impromptu picnic. It's not until the dumpster crew is safely inside for coffee and a sweet treat that Daisy and I get on with evicting the Trash Pandas.

In the end, it's a decidedly lopsided cup cake that does the trick. One whiff and the little critters march up the boards I'd had put in place, given how deep that thing was.

The challenge now is what to do with them. It's illegal to have them as pets, despite Daisy being all for it. What she doesn't need is the damage they can cause if left to their own devices.

Before we've come to any decisions, they've finished their morning tea and are off up the oak tree without a backward glance. It's a problem for later.

But with that diversion out of the way, it's time to deal with Daisy's determination to stay here.

THIRTEEN

DAISY

I'm still angry at Josh and his resolve to have me moving out while we deal with whoever wants to buy the building. Well, no longer. I'm taking ownership in full. No scummy property developer is forcing me out.

I'm all too conscious that I'm paying a mortgage while not earning a bean. The sooner I can have The Daisy Chain back up and running, the better my finances will be. I can't afford anymore hold ups.

And with that in mind, I shut myself in the small office, determined to order signage for the front of the shop. While the sign Josh had helped me remove at the old place is lovely, it's far too small for the façade of the large Victorian building.

It's difficult concentrating, though, with the team kicking up a heck of a noise as they set about fitting a make-shift sprinkler system. A quick look had told me there's nothing pretty about this, but then it's not destined to stay.

Once we've dealt with the property developer, we can safely remove it and patch any holes left behind. And I say 'we', with Ethan and the others just as determined to deal with whoever's behind the attacks as I am.

Despite Lucky Break being caught up simply because of Rod Baker's involvement, Ethan is still angry about it. And it's not just about his company's reputation, but his love of old buildings.

I guess with him having been brought up by his grandfather at The Laurels; it makes sense. Add in that these days he lives at Eagle's Nest on the cliffs north of town, and it was a given.

The team works hard throughout the day, although not on the renovations. These are on hold until we've dealt with our developer friend. I'm itching to know who's behind these attacks, with it obvious I'm not alone in being targeted.

There'd been no missing the sadness in old Mr. Brettell's eyes at him shutting up shop. I doubt, given the option, he'd have done so, but being in business was hard enough these days. Add in some asshat targeting you with petty vandalism, and it became a nightmare.

Much as I want to talk to some other local businesses, Cole had said he didn't think it was a good idea. "It wouldn't fit in with you wanting to sell."

And he's right. If I'm to pretend that I've had enough and just want out, no matter the price, then I'll need to tread carefully. Especially once the FOR-SALE sign goes up.

Come six that evening and while Ethan has gone home, a lot of the team is still on site. As they crawl all over the building, they're dragging various lengths of perforated tubing behind them. This is a clear plastic, meaning it won't stand out as much as it would if it were black.

Along with this activity, members of the team have been taking time out to sit in their vehicles. They've been keeping a close eye on anyone driving by more than once, or even anyone on foot who was taking too much interest in The Daisy Chain.

Thankfully, it's all been quiet on that front, meaning the installation of the sprinkler system has mostly gone unnoticed. At least, this is the hope.

There's no sign of the team slowing down, or indeed going home, with them even ordering in pizza. This had me wracked with guilt, with Ethan having told me he wouldn't be charging for this extra work.

The least I could have done was provide dinner for his team. Meanwhile, Josh had rustled up a meal for us, with him proving himself to be quite the cook with rough-and-ready meals.

But, for Ethan and the crew who've worked with Rod Baker in the past, this is personal. It doesn't matter that their ex-workmate was simply a cog in someone else's machinations. They've hated seeing their company targeted.

According to Josh, a few of the team have records of the type that make it hard for them to find employment. However, it was something Ethan was prepared to look past, so long as they kept to the straight and narrow.

Right after dinner, three of the men slip out of the back door, ready to spend the night in the tents they'd pitched earlier. They're yawning widely when they pass through the kitchen, a testament to the effort they'd put in during the day.

Meanwhile, Cole and Malakai are camping in the shop, while the small office is once again home to Zac and Spencer. The one thing they all have in common is that they look capable of anything the developer and his dodgy friends can throw up.

This leaves Josh and me, with him still not happy that I've opted to stay rather than return to the apartment over the garage at Chase and Josie's place. However, when we climb into bed up in the attic, after leaving the others to finish their dinner, all that is forgotten.

There's something magical about the space at the top of the house, imbued as it is with Josh and his memories of childhood. Tucked up in his arms, I feel safe and cared for. And knowing there's a veritable army downstairs doesn't go astray.

"Do you think it'll work?" Despite my being fully into Skye's idea of fake selling the place, what if someone else tries to buy it? It's something I ask before Josh has answered my first question.

He stays quiet, although I get that it's because he's thinking of his reply rather than he doesn't want to answer. "You could say you're selling because of the attacks. Say you want to be open and honest about this because of the danger involved."

"That makes sense. If it's anyone other than our guy, they'd run a mile, surely? Unless they're another property developer."

The way Ethan had talked, it sounded as if there was more than one. But could they all be as devious as the one after The Daisy Chain?

As if sensing my disquiet, Josh's hand settles on my tummy, dampening the butterflies. "So, tell me, what will The Daisy Chain be like when you open?"

It's the perfect diversion. Any thoughts of the building being a smoldering pile are soon replaced with images of a shop filled to bursting with colorful blooms.

"Oh, it's going to be wonderful." I go through the many flowers I'll have in stock, and of the colored paper and ribbon I'll use for bouquets. I'm fully into it when the crashing realization hits me that Josh won't be able to see any of that.

My hand settles over his, and I squeeze it tight. "I'm so sorry. I didn't think."

And I hadn't. Color is such an integral part of my life that I've never stopped to think it was something others couldn't share. Even thinking about a world without color is enough to dampen my enthusiasm about my new shop.

"That's okay, Daze. There's more to life than color, there really is." His hand slips from under mine, working its way down my body to rest between my legs. "For example, my sense of smell is off the charts." He breathes deeply through his nose before carrying on. "And that tells me you're wet with need."

When his fingers slip between my curls, this is confirmed. Oh, so wet. My head sinks into the pillow as I blossom under his touch, with my body knowing exactly what it wants. Even better is that Josh knows this, too.

JOSH

All thoughts of color dissolve as I take my fill of the glorious image of Daisy spread out under me.

Sure, it would be wonderful to see the colors as nature intended, but it wasn't all bad. Even with the limitations of my colorblindness, Daisy's skin glows under the icicle lights.

And hell, she smells amazing. The musk of her arousal, combined with the floral perfume she favors, is a heady mix. I'm taking my full of her giving into another shattering climax when the icicle lights first flicker, and then die.

It was only a matter of time. I'm surprised they've lasted as long as they have. Something that won't last any longer is me, with Daisy's sheath milking my length in waves. It's enough to have me over the edge in a climax strong enough that I'm still seeing lights.

It's when I'm drawing in desperately needed air that I notice something else, and it's not the musk of our lovemaking. For a second, I think it's down to whichever icicle light had blown.

Another sniff and I know there's no way something that small could cause this strong a smell.

"Daisy, we need to move." There's nothing delicate about my withdrawal, with her gasping in protest. "Sorry, sweetheart, but I smell smoke."

As dark as it is, I'm not sure what she makes of this, but when I rip the blanket down off the window, I see that she's in shock. Once I look down into the backyard, I'm in a similar state.

"What the hell?" I can't say anymore than this, my mind crowded with questions. Top of which is where the heck are the others? Despite the tents in the backyard reflecting the fire inside the building, there's no movement from any of them.

I don't get it; we didn't even have beer with dinner. Something is off, in a big way. I'm soon dragging my jeans on commando style and grabbing my t-shirt before stumbling over to the stairs.

As dark as it is, I turn on the torch on my phone and take my time, all too conscious of Daisy stumbling around as she rushes to get dressed. My worst fears are confirmed when, at the bottom of the stairs, I see smoke seeping around the edges of the panel.

I touch it cautiously, immediately yanking my hand back. The wood is hot enough to have it close to igniting. After yelling out, "Daisy, don't come down here." I retrace my steps.

Back up in the attic, while Daisy phones 911, I first call Cole, and then Malakai. Neither of them answers. I don't get it. Ethan is the only one to answer, with him nowhere near close enough to help.

After yelling that he's on his way, he hangs up on me. Another check of the tents in the backyard shows me nothing has changed.

"Where the hell are they? They should have turned on the sprinklers by now."

Daisy, who's busy giving details to the emergency dispatcher, looks at me, her eyes wide with terror. They widen further still, before she briefly tips the phone away from her mouth. "The pizza?"

Thanks to my mind being flooded with worry about how we'll escape, I don't immediately understand the import of what she's said. And while the cogs are slow to turn, they eventually slip into place.

When the guys ordered pizza for dinner, I already had ours underway, so we'd stayed with that. Could it be they've all come down with food poisoning?

As horrific as the idea of the men downstairs being at the mercy of the fire, was that of Daisy and me being trapped up here.

The temperature was steadily rising, with beads of sweat forming on my forehead. The acrid smell of burning wood and plastic filled my nostrils, enough that rather than put my t-shirt on, I wrap it around my face. It would be better if it was wet, but anything will help.

As soon as I've got myself organized, I help Daisy with a make-shift mask of her own. It's the best we can do, even if a tiny part of my brain tells me it's pointless, that we're toast.

Damn it, I've finally met a woman who doesn't make me feel less of a man because of my stupid eyesight. This can't be how it ends, it just can't.

And yet, that sliding panel had been scorching hot to the touch, telling me the flames had already engulfed a significant portion of the building. The crackling sound of burning debris echoed through the attic, adding to my overall sense of chaos and panic.

I'm back next to the window, calculating how badly we'd be hurt if we were to jump, when I think of something else. That the attic had been untouched said the owners after my grandparents hadn't known about it. Could the same be true for the blocked-off part?

After holding my finger up to show a terrified Daisy that I've thought of something, I jog over to the staircase. However, I don't use it, with the narrow stairwell now a guaranteed death trap.

Rather, I clamber onto the ancient bookcase, sending my childhood toys flying. From there, I flip open the hatch grandpa and I installed when we closed up this part of the attic to keep the heating bills down.

On using my phone to light the space, I'm relieved to see the enormous old water tank is still there. Back in the day, this was what pressurized the water for the building, although it was always sluggish.

I know it's a long shot that it will be full, but we're short of options here. Even a couple of inches in the bottom could make a difference. After smacking my hand against the side of the tank, I'm rewarded with a dull thud rather than a solid boom. I repeat the process higher up. Holy moly, she's close to full.

There has to be near on a couple of hundred gallons in that thing. If I can just tip it on its side and send it down through the middle of the building, it might do the trick. It might even douse the flames enough for Daisy and me to escape.

To sit and do nothing isn't an option. Despite the fire station being nearby, the heat of that panel was such that I doubt we'll last long enough for the firefighters to arrive in time to rescue us.

Rather than get down using the bookcase, I jump and make my way over to Daisy. I then take her by the hand and lead her back the way I'd come. "Sweetheart, I need your help. You'll have to put the call on speakerphone."

It's at this point I realize she's as good as frozen, hardly able to comprehend anything beyond the calming voice of the emergency dispatcher. In the end, I take the phone off her, flip it to speaker and put it atop the bookcase.

I'm not sure if it's adrenaline or desperation, but I soon have her through the hatch, with me right behind her. Rather than leave the dispatcher in the dark, between grunts of exertion, I've been yelling a blow-by-blow commentary.

I don't care how many times she says the fire engines are on their way; I refuse to sit around and do nothing. After getting Daisy to sit with her back to the water tank, I join her.

It's going to take our combined efforts to tip this thing over, if it's even possible. Either way, anything has to be better than sitting there calmly waiting for your demise. If I go out, it won't be with a whimper.

"Daze, this thing is full. If we can shove it over, it might kill the fire."

At last, I see an ounce of sanity in her gaze, with her then putting her feet next to mine on a huge header beam. It would be better if we were wearing shoes, but in the panic, mine are still under the bed somewhere. I suspect the same is true of hers.

"Okay, on three. Ready? One! Two!! Three!!!"

We straighten our legs, our backs jammed into the water tank, both of us straining and giving it all we've got. And nothing. The damned thing doesn't move an inch. This can't be happening, it just can't.

FOURTEEN

DAISY

Adrenaline floods my body in a powerful surge, washing away the panic that had me nearly frozen. My heart pounds with a deafening thump that's easily as loud as the crackle of the fire somewhere below.

To calm myself, I greedily inhale as much air as my make-shift mask will allow. However, this results in me coughing uncontrollably, the harsh sound bouncing around us. Josh slapping my back only intensifies my response, with me eventually waving him away.

Only by breathing deeply and slowly through my nose am I able to fight the urge to cough. I can breathe as much fresh air as I want once we escape. And for that to happen, I need to focus.

I don't want to die up here with this wonderful man.

And while I've always dreamed about having someone that I love next to me when that happened, this wasn't exactly how I saw things going.

I'm still struggling with the realization that I love him intensely when he yells, "Let's stand! We'll have more leverage that way.!"

There's no missing the desperation in his voice with this spurring me into action. As awkward as it is, I stand with his help, alarmed to feel how warm the rough boards now are under my feet.

This, as much as Josh's urging, has me shoving that darn tank as hard as I can. Hard enough that I'm sure I've dislocated my shoulder.

All that is forgotten when the tank lurches slowly away from us. When it rocks back into place, there's nothing I can do to stop the sob that bursts free. However, rather than be defeated as I am, Josh crows in triumph.

"Again! Harder next time!"

"Again? Harder?" My response to his encouragement is weak. All I can hope is that my efforts to topple the tank aren't as pathetic.

I ready myself to give it my all. This time, instead of using my other shoulder, I once again put my back against the tank, taking comfort in how cool it still is.

With the large beam I'm using for leverage now inexorably hotter beneath my bare feet, this time when Josh yells, "Push!" I give it my all. And then some, my legs and core screaming with the effort.

For a horrifying moment, I think nothing has happened, with the sensation of falling confusing me. That is until Josh reaches out and grabs me at the last minute, yanking me away from the gaping hole caused by the slowly toppling tank.

In our favor, is that when it hits the floor below, it ruptures, with water exploding in all directions. Josh and I are drenched, with me taking comfort in its cooling effects.

More comforting than this is the loud hiss that comes from the floor below. It's only once we know we won't get caught in an updraft of flame that we risk peering into the void.

It's pitch black down there, meaning we can't see a darn thing. Which is marvelous, with there also being no telltale signs of fire. However, the smoke that soon billows out of the hole is enough to have us backing off and through the hatch to the main attic floor.

After hurrying to get our shoes on, we stand in front of the windows. While I twist the lever to unlock the double-hung window on my side of the large central pane, Josh does the same on his. I yank on the window and nothing happens other than me hurting my shoulder again.

No! The window's been painted shut, with the same apparently true of the one Josh is cussing over.

"Damn it! We don't have time for this! Stand back!" Josh grabs the apple crate from next to the bed and, without pause, smashes it through the central pane. While I'm devastated at the loss of the beautiful rippled glass, the delicious night air now rolling in makes up for it. Standing as close as we dare to the large jagged hole, we suck on the life-giving oxygen, all while clinging to each other.

Eventually, we hear sirens in the distance. And while they're closing in, they'd never have been here in time to save us. I give up the fight to hold my tears at bay, with them soon streaming down my face unbidden.

"Hey, there, Daze. You're okay. You're going to be okay." Josh continues to hold me tight, the steady beat of his heart and the rise and fall of his chest calming me as much as his whispered encouragement.

I never want him to let me go. Burying my face against his powerful body, I take comfort in his raw strength. If I'd been up here on my own, I'd never have made it out alive.

Then I hear something over the strong beat of his heart. It's a disembodied voice. Is it someone downstairs? I tip my head to the side and listen intently.

There it is again. "Are you okay? Are you there? Hello!" Whoever it is, they're getting increasingly desperate.

I soon realize it's the emergency dispatcher, with my 911 call still open. Through her we're able to direct the fire crew to our whereabouts with a ladder soon appearing through the hole caused by the water tank.

On my way down the ladder, I take one last look at the attic, and can do nothing about the shudder that traverses my frame. Despite the happy times I've spent up there with Josh, I never want to see the place again.

When I finally step foot on the first floor, the true scale of the devastation is brought home. I'm still dealing with this and how close Josh and I had come to dying, when the fire chief plants himself in front of us.

"We'll need to carry out a full investigation. I trust we can count on your co-operation."

I'm not sure if it's how he said it, but I didn't like that his statement reeked of 'insurance fraud'. And while he might be right that the fire looks to be suspicious, as close as I'd come to dying, I let him have it. This, more than Josh holding me tight, went a long way to ridding me of the terror that still had me in its grip.

I'm still bristling with indignation when I catch sight of firefighters giving oxygen to the Lucky Break team who'd been caught inside. Water dripping from the floor above, smoke hanging in the air, and the glare of flashlights give the scene a nightmarish quality.

"Chief, you just work out how it started. We could have died up there!"

As the words escape my lips, their weight in my throat and the bitterness of the truth are brought home in dramatic fashion. Once again, my tears get the better of me, with my body shaking because of their intensity.

I'm hardly aware of Josh swinging me up into his arms and marching through the shop and out onto the sidewalk. He doesn't get much farther when he realizes that the keys to his truck are up in the attic.

"I just want to get you away from here."

He's barely finished stating this when a truck pulls up in front of us. Chase Hunter is at the wheel, with Josie next to him. My friend tumbles from the truck, desperate to see if I'm alright.

She's doing her best to hug me, which has Josh reluctantly lowering me to the ground. My feet have barely touched the sidewalk when Josie wraps me in a crushing embrace.

"When Ethan phoned, I couldn't believe it." She looks briefly at the building behind us, before again examining me as if searching for burns. "Are you sure that you're okay?"

Despite me doing my best to convince her I'm fine, she's determined to take me back to The Laurels.

I don't want to leave, but there's not much I can do if I stay. Tomorrow, though, will be a different story. If the fire had been deliberately lit, as everyone suspects, then we need to find out who was behind it.

After making Josh promise to collect me first thing in the morning, I allow him to bundle me into the back of the truck. Despite Chase and Josie being eager to get me back to their place, I take the time to kiss him goodnight.

It's a kiss that's brimming with thanks as much as passion. I owe my life to this wonderful and caring man. Because of the time crunch, I don't think twice when I whisper, "Thank you, my love," after breaking the kiss.

We're pulling slowly away, with me staring at Josh through the back window of the cab, when Ethan arrives. There is no missing that the boss of Lucky

Break Construction is angry. And who can blame him? Even if the fire proves to be accidental, he came close to losing four or five of his men tonight.

JOSH

It's daybreak before I'm close to being able to leave The Daisy Chain. During the night, I'd watched as Ethan had taken Cole and Malakai to the hospital for observation. Out of everyone, they'd been hit the hardest with smoke inhalation.

I'd also found the electricity had been deliberately cut, further adding to our suspicions. While I'd thought the icicle lights had finally died because of their advanced years, this hadn't been the case.

Even if the guys had been woken by the fire, the sprinkler system wouldn't have worked. Not with electric pumps necessary to pressurize the water enough for it to make it to the upper levels.

I still don't understand how the guys inside the building could have slept through both the break-in and the fire. I'd asked them if they'd come down with food poisoning, as Daisy suspected, but this hadn't been the case. Rather, they'd mentioned being bone tired, but that was all.

With nothing left to do on site, I find a ladder and scramble back up to the attic. As well as collecting the keys to my truck, I grab mine and Daisy's bags, unsure if the contents have been smoke-damaged. I guess we'll find out soon enough.

It's not much past eight o'clock when I drive through the gates at The Laurels, the mansion that Josie and Chase Hunter call home. After following the driveway around back and parking by the triple-car garage, I plod up the stairs at the side.

My knock is tentative. For all I know, Daisy could still be fast asleep after the events of last night. I'm therefore taken by surprise when she immediately wrenches the door open and throws herself into my arms, clinging tight.

Even better is when she drags me inside and starts removing my clothes. However, it's not so she can have her way with me, although this only becomes apparent when she leads me through to the bathroom and turns on the shower.

Next thing I know, she's shoving me under a stream of scalding hot water and handing me a sponge. A look down at my naked form and I can see why. I'm covered in soot, the black streaks that mar my arms and chest close to obscuring my blue and green tattoos.

A quick check of the mirror over the vanity and I can see my face hasn't escaped the aftermath of the fire, either. Last night could have ended so badly for all of us. It's a sobering thought that has me simply standing there, letting the water pummel me.

"Josh, come on. You need to clean up. We've got a lot to do."

It's hearing the determination in her voice that has me looking at her properly. There's a hardness to her dark blue eyes that I've not seen before. It doesn't bode well for whomever was potentially behind the fire, with a property developer, the most likely candidate.

As tired as I am, I'm suddenly imbued with a similar determination. Whoever they are, they're not getting away with it. Not while there's breath in my body.

Damn it, he'd come close to killing the woman I love. It's a realization that has me immediately lost to my surroundings. My mind instead bursting with how wonderful a life with Daisy could be.

While the shower does a lot to revive me, this is nothing compared to walking into the main room of the apartment and finding she's whipped up breakfast. There's also a fresh brew of coffee that looks to be industrial in strength.

I'll need it if I'm to keep upright. I'd vowed when leaving the building earlier that I wouldn't sleep until I'd worked out who was behind the fire. Well, not until that night, at the very least. While I was determined to solve the mystery, I wasn't a complete idiot.

There's nothing leisurely about our breakfast, with Daisy raring to go. Honestly, I'd have expected her to be more tired after so little sleep. I guess with her out for justice, she's on edge.

"Josh, we need to be at Tremaine Hardware as soon as they open. I want to get the biggest FOR-SALE BY OWNER sign they've got."

In the end, we get there a couple of minutes before opening, with Daisy bouncing from foot to foot in her eagerness to get inside. And damn if I don't love her even more for it.

The signs are down at the very back of the store. The dust coating the one on top of the pile says they're not a big seller. The only thing that's big is the sign that Daisy opts for.

It's enormous. Big enough that when she holds it up so I can have a proper look, all that shows of my gorgeous, brave girl are her hands and feet.

"That should do it, Daze. If it was that scummy developer who started the fire, there's no way he'll miss that!"

I'm about to take it off her when my phone rings.

A quick look at the screen and I see that it's Ethan. "What gives?"

I don't need to say anything else with him recounting what it was Lindsey had discovered after phoning around her book club members. No need for a meeting when a phone call would suffice.

After ending the call, I reach for the sign. "Daisy, have you ever heard of a guy called Trevor Thom? He owns Triple-T Investments."

She only thinks about it briefly before answering. "No, can't say I have. Why do you ask?"

As we make our way to the checkouts, I recount my conversation with my boss. "According to someone Lindsey spoke to, that's who's been buying up the properties in your area."

With a name to go on, she's more determined than ever to catch the guy. Back at The Daisy Chain, rather than go inside and inspect the damage, she insists I get a hammer and nails from my truck.

Thus armed, she erects the sign herself, coming close to smashing her fingers while she's about it. It doesn't matter that it's not level, it should still work.

The last thing she does is to pull a marker pen from the back pocket of her no-nonsense overalls and write NEGOTIABLE in large letters next to the dollar sign.

After unlocking the front doors and walking inside, I'm able to confirm the damage isn't as bad as it could have been. From outside, it's hard to see any at all. It's doubtless for this reason that Daisy's shaken when she stops next to me. After squeezing her eyes shut, she grips my arm tight enough I actually wince.

"Daze, it's not as bad as it looks. Really." After gently breaking her death grip on my forearm, I take her hand and lead her through the doorway at the back of the shop and into the small hallway.

Her hand tightening on mine when she sees the damage to the staircase lets me know she hasn't bought into my optimism. "Okay, okay, so it doesn't look great. But because they used old-growth wood to build this place, it's mostly charred."

Conscious of her shock, I wrap my arms around her and hold her tight, hoping to absorb her distress. I also take relief in her nearness. Last night could have ended so badly, the very thought enough to have me fighting off a shudder. The realization I could have lost Daisy in the fire is like a punch to the gut.

To have her focusing on something more positive, I voice the next rational thought that comes to mind. "Of course, we'll need to get an engineer in to make sure there's no structural damage. But all-in-all, it's not as bad as it could have been."

With us in a holding pattern until we find out how the fire started and who was responsible, there's no point in tidying up. And if that Triple-T guy is behind it, as Ethan suspects, Daisy will have to convince him she just wants to be done with the place. For him to believe that, she'll have to act that way.

We're still standing wrapped in each other's arms when a taxi pulls up out front. However, rather than it be the developer, it's Malakai and Cole. While the men appear to be clean, the same can't be said of their clothes, telling us they've come straight from the hospital.

Without so much as a hello, Malakai leads the charge, his phone already in his hand. A couple of swipes and he finds what it is he's looking for. When he plays us some grainy black and white security footage of a guy breaking in, shock prickles my scalp.

"We need to show this to the police." Daisy's words are barely above a whisper.

And while her response doesn't surprise me, Cole, backing her up, brings home just how cold-blooded last night's attack had been.

From what I know of the older guy, he'd usually be happier dealing with things himself, not calling the authorities.

FIFTEEN

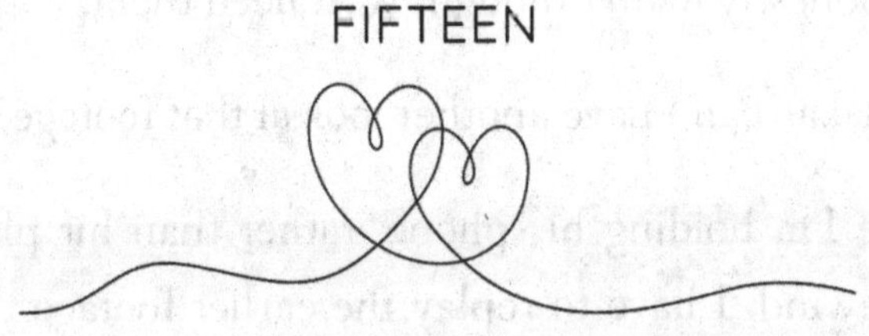

DAISY

As I wait in the backyard under the large oak with Malakai, Cole, and Josh for the police to arrive, I'm struggling to come to terms with everything.

Even worse than the guy setting fire to the building was that he knew there were people inside when he did so. The footage proved that beyond doubt.

What I still don't understand is why the men had slept through the break in. He'd have to have made some sound, no matter how careful he was.

And he'd entered through the front doors, which meant he'd had to have stepped over Cole and

Malakai before starting the fire at the bottom of the stairs. But with no cameras inside, we'd never know. We honestly hadn't thought we'd need them.

"Malakai, can I have another look at that footage?"

Once I'm holding his phone, rather than hit play, I hit rewind. I have to replay the earlier footage three times before I see what's wrong. The guy who'd delivered the pizza hadn't been wearing a uniform.

Josh, who's looking over my shoulder as I lean back against him, sees something else entirely. "Daze, can you go back a couple of minutes earlier?"

Now Cole and Malakai are also crowding around me, with them blocking out the sun, making it even easier to see the recording. If Josh hadn't pointed it out, I'd never have seen it.

To me, it was nothing more than some indistinct gray blurs. However, when Malakai played with the settings and zoomed in on the top right corner, there it was.

After parking his van and getting out, the pizza delivery driver had been intercepted by a guy carrying a fully laden, white plastic bag. Whoever the second guy was, he'd handed something over.

No doubt money, with this always talking.

Now in possession of the stack of pizza boxes, the stranger had dropped them on the doorstep of The Daisy Chain, along with the plastic bag. After a quick knock, he'd hurried away. Unfortunately, with him having his head down and a cap pulled low, there was no way of identifying him.

"No way was that legit." While I've said this out loud, the rest of my reasoning had been internal. I mean, what are the chances that the guy with the bag of sodas would know the team had ordered pizza?

"Malakai? The pizza last night?"

I don't have time to say anything else, with Cole guffawing loudly and interrupting me. "Like this one would ever spring for dinner!"

After glaring briefly at Cole, Malakai looks at me, an interesting mix of confusion and embarrassment. "Yeah, sorry, we meant to say thanks last night, but you'd already gone to bed."

Now it's my turn to be confused, with Josh in a similar state.

"What do you mean?" I address my question to Malakai before turning to look at Cole over my shoulder. "Sorry, but I didn't order pizza. Honestly, by the time I thought about that, it had already been delivered."

It's Cole who catches on before any of us. "Huh, I guess that explains why the soda wasn't as fizzy as it should have been."

As sheltered a life as I've led, he has to spell it out for me. Without that, I'd never have known it was possible to inject something through the cap of a soda bottle while leaving the twist seal intact.

We've come to no conclusions about what to do with this information when the police arrive, calling out to us from inside.

I'm so pleased to see it is Detective Johnson and Officer Ramirez, the two we'd talked to at the station. Better them than the team that visited after the first attack. That pair would be as likely to give us a lecture on the dangers of smoking.

Once we join them, we don't bother going through everything in painstaking detail. Instead, Malakai shows the officers the footage of the sodas being added to the pizza delivery. And like Cole, the pair picks up quickly enough that Cole and the others must have been drugged.

You'd think all their Christmases had come at once when they hear Cole and Malakai had ended up in the hospital for observation overnight.

"And they took blood and urine samples?" If the situation weren't as serious, the anticipation on the Detective's face would have me giggling.

I'm surprised when the men nod in unison, with my having thought they'd be given oxygen, and that'd be it. But apparently the other tests could show just how badly the smoke had affected them.

Detective Johnson, a grim smile in place, nods briefly to his partner. Without saying another word, the junior officer leaves the shop, making his way over to a decrepit car parked on the other side of the road.

On seeing my surprise, the detective explains it doesn't always pay to drive around in the nicest car. Even at this distance, I see Ramirez is on the radio. It's not a long conversation, with him soon back inside, a brief smile to his boss in acknowledgement.

Malakai hits the play button again, taking the officers through the footage of the guy when he breaks in. While there was something weighing down the front pocket of his jacket when he arrived, when he left, it was no longer there.

It was Officer Ramirez who picked up what the rest of us had missed.

"Same guy as delivered the pizza. See the limp."

And he's right. While it wasn't too obvious, once you were on the lookout, there was no missing it.

We're getting to where the officers ask that we head down to the station so we can complete official paperwork, when a Mercedes pulls up out front. It's Josh who reacts, stiffening next to me.

"What is it?"

He leans over, his mouth deliciously close to my ear. "That car, it was parked in the background on the footage from the camera."

Without waiting, he hustles the two police officers down the hallway and into the small office. Them having overheard his comment; they comply without issue. Next thing I know is that Cole and Malakai have shot through to the kitchen, leaving Josh and me alone in the shop.

As I watch the guy walk up and stand outside the front doors, there's no missing that limp. I've never been more nervous in my life. Actually, that's not true. I'd been more nervous when this guy tried to barbeque me last night.

This has me straightening my spine, my resolve bolstered by knowing there are two police officers not ten feet from me.

Rather than come inside, the guy taps the large FOR-SALE sign.

"I see you're wanting to sell."

Unable to speak, I nod woodenly.

"And you're negotiable?"

When I again nod, there's no missing the avarice glinting in his eyes or the smug little smile he indulges in.

Then, channeling every school play I was ever unlucky enough to take part in, I wring my hands, doing my best to tamp down the melodrama. "I don't want to, but the project has gotten out of hand."

Courtesy of any further words being jammed in my throat, I instead gesture to the side in a silent invitation for him to enter. I probably needn't have bothered with him more than ready to come in, declare the place a write-off, and offer me a pittance.

As focused as I am on the guy now standing in the middle of my shop, I'm not taking as much notice of Josh as I should.

However, the merest glance to the side is enough to see he's got his phone out. Whether this is to record our conversation or call for help, I'm not sure.

I'm therefore thrown when he drops his phone in the bib pocket of my overalls and walks toward the developer.

When he doesn't take the chance to punch the guy in the nose, but walks around him and out the front doors, I'm disappointed, and then nervous.

Deciding I'd rather be closer to the officers, I lead the way through into the hallway, stopping next to the stairs and the worst of the fire damage.

Rather than retracing his steps, Josh is peering in the back window of the Mercedes, something obviously having caught his eye. I'd much rather he was in here with me, because I don't like how this creep is invading my personal space.

It's enough to have me taking a big step back, ready to yell for help if needs be. He's opening his mouth, no doubt to start on his rehearsed spiel, when I beat him to it.

"I feel I need to be honest with you." After pausing for dramatic effect, I press on. "The fire wasn't accidental. It was arson."

"I don't care. That's no problem for me." His words have been rushed, as if he can't get them out soon enough. He follows this up by grabbing a business card from the inside pocket of his jacket and thrusting it at me.

A glance is enough to catch Triple-T Investments in stark red and I come close to dropping the card, my fingers lacking any power. My heart is now hammering to the point I'm sure he'll hear it. "But aren't you worried they'll target you, too ..." I take another look at the card. "Mr. Thom?"

He's now shaking his head so hard that if he was wearing a wig, it'd be gone by now. "No, no. I'm all good with that." When he then offers me half of what I paid for it, it takes every ounce of my self-control not to smack him.

First, he tries to kill me, and now he's trying to rip me off. Seriously?

"Is it alright if I think about it? I know there was someone else who was interested when I bought it. Maybe I should talk to them first?"

If I'd thought he was crowding me before, it's nothing compared to now, his face mere inches from mine. "If you know what's good for you, Ms. Green, you'll sell it to me. It would be too bad if something were to happen to you. If there was, I don't know, say another fire."

I'm wondering where the heck Josh is when the door to the small office opens behind the guy without him noticing. Oh no, he's too busy threatening me with another fire to notice that.

When Detective Johnson looks at me and lifts an eyebrow, I take a second to work out what he's after. "Oh, right?" I then hold the business card up so he can read the name on it.

So much easier to read someone their Miranda Rights when you knew their name.

JOSH

As loath as I'd been to leave Daisy alone with that guy, I knew he'd never threaten her in front of me. I also knew that when he did so, it would be within earshot of the two officers hiding in the small office.

I wasn't leaving it there though, making sure I hit the video function on my phone before sliding it into the bib pocket on her overalls. Even better was that the pocket was small enough for my phone to poke out of the top.

All going well, we'll get both sound and pictures.

I'd been tempted to open a live feed, but worried about getting my ass sued. That guy didn't get as rich as he apparently was by playing nicely. He was also the sort to have a team of attorneys on speed dial.

With Malakai and Cole hiding in the kitchen, there was never any danger to Daisy, although it wouldn't have felt that way to her. Despite my barely speaking to the guy, I got he was nasty to the core.

The type who wouldn't think twice about setting fire to a building full of people. Anything to seal the deal was how Ethan had put it when he'd phoned me.

All of this had been to a background of Mr. Triple T spluttering about his rights, and him being a leader in the community. When he'd added that the mayor was a close friend, I think that was the final straw for Ramirez.

Everyone knew the mayor wasn't as squeaky clean as he'd like people to believe.

Certainly, the alleged friendship had no effect on the officers, with them sticking to the rules, including making us leave the building when they did. The doors had then been locked, with Daisy handing her key to them. I'd followed suit with the key she'd had cut for Lucky Break Construction.

It was better if the cops knew no-one could enter until they returned. And anyway, it wasn't as if there was anything of value inside, unless you counted my camping gear.

On watching Detective Johnson and Officer Ramirez driving away, with the crooked developer safely tucked up in the back, I'm flooded with relief.

Even if by some miracle that creep escapes without conviction, by then it will be too late, with any investors having moved on, or distanced themselves.

Coogan's Break was too small to avoid rumors completely.

The last thing Daisy had told the police before they'd left was about Mr. Brettell next door and him being forced out of his property.

When I'd added that they should also check the developer's Mercedes, they'd at first looked at me strangely. "There's a can of black spray paint on the floor in the back."

Malakai had then taken up the baton. "I'd say the chances are that it's an exact match for that used to black out several of our security cameras."

Obviously, we'll all need to make official statements, but better if we give the cops something to go on in the meantime. On the cop car turning the corner, I squeeze Daisy briefly before picking her up and spinning her around.

"You know what this means?"

Rather than answer, she laughs delightedly, the sound wonderful to hear. It's in stark contrast to the worry that's hounded her. The only problem now is the work site is officially a crime scene, meaning that all of us are technically out of work.

We're still discussing our options when Ethan arrives, with us soon bringing him fully up to speed.

"Sorry Daisy, but that means no work until this is sorted out. We can't afford to mess up any evidence."

There's no missing her disappointment at this being confirmed. "No, no, I understand."

With nothing else to be done, and Ethan heading home to rustle up more work for us, I bundle Daisy into my truck. Where we're going, I wouldn't have a clue. While I can take her back to the apartment over the garage at The Laurels, I can't stay there. Not at my boss's brother's place. That'd be all kinds of weird.

Only when we're sitting in the cab ready to leave, do I turn to her. "Would you like to go back to my place?" I know it's a corny line, with Daisy bursting out laughing in response proving this beyond all doubt.

However, rather than give me further grief about it, she simply answers, "I thought you'd never ask."

When I put my truck in gear and we take off, she's still giggling, with me deciding I like this new carefree version.

I suspect this will change when reality sinks in that it might be months before she can get The Daisy Chain up and running. Months during which she'll still have to cover mortgage payments.

On turning into the driveway at my place, I'm nervous to the point my hands slip on the steering wheel and I hit the edge of the curb. While Daisy won't be the first woman who's been here, her opinion of my home means more than that of any other.

I'm not worried about opening the front door and finding a pair of dirty socks on the couch. I'm too much of a clean freak for that. It's for this reason the lawns are freshly mowed, and the small bushes on either side of the door, neatly trimmed.

No, my nerves are because I'm worried about what she'll think of the color scheme, or lack thereof. After getting out of the truck, I fidget with my keys, trying to delay the moment of truth.

As Daisy looks around, taking in the simple ranch house, her expression speaks volumes, with her words soon backing this up. "Wow, it's, ah, immaculate."

Though this could be taken as a compliment, I get there's more to it. Only then do I look at my place with fresh eyes. Yes, it's tidy. It's also insipid. That in worrying about messing up my colors, I'd avoided any.

We walk up to the front door, and I fumble with the lock, finally opening it. After we step inside, Daisy is strangely quiet. Sadly, the interior is just as bland as the exterior, with everything white, or failing that, black.

Compared to the attic at The Daisy Chain, my home lacks character; it lacks a soul. Damn it, how could I have let my stupid eyesight rule my life like this? Even if I stuck to colors that I knew worked together, it'd be better than this glorified monk's cell.

Eventually, I can stand the silence no longer. Turning to Daisy, I take her hands in mine and give them a gentle squeeze. "Can you help me?"

She looks up at me, her confusion clear.

"Color. This place needs color."

On catching the strange light in her eyes, I wonder if I haven't just unleashed a monster. When she speaks, I know I have.

"Oh, I can see it now." She turns her head slowly in one direction, and then in the other, her gaze eventually settling on the blank wall at the end of the lounge. "You could make that a feature wall. Perhaps use some wallpaper. You like flowers, don't you?"

She's right about this. I do like flowers, although the daisy is my favorite. In particular, this Daisy.

"You're right, I do like flowers." I want to say more, but I'm worried it's too soon. We've only known each other for a few weeks, and yet it's as if I've known her my entire life. Or is it I've been dreaming of a woman like her since I decided girls weren't icky? "Do you think you could help me with it?"

Her response is immediate. She throws herself at me, and we tumble onto the couch, our bodies intertwined.

"Oh, Josh," she murmurs. "I'd love to help you." And then she seals the deal with a kiss that leaves me in no doubt.

When she eventually pulls away, the room is no longer as sterile, with it feeling as if I'm already surrounded by a burst of color. And with Daisy by my side, I am.

Now all I need to do is convince her to stay.

SIXTEEN

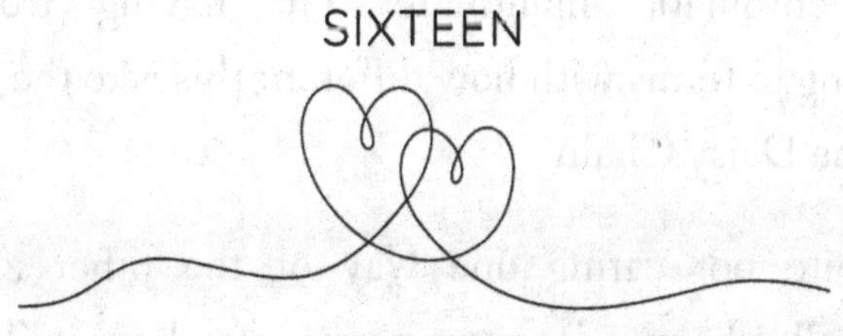

DAISY

I'm not sure what I expected of Josh's home, but this doesn't come close. While he can be a grumpy so-and-so, he's also got a kind heart.

In sharp contrast, his home—make that house—lacks any at all. And this doesn't stop with the lounge, the same being true of the dining room, kitchen and even the bathroom.

White, so much white. And while there are occasional accents of black, these are an affront, rather than a relief. As unexpected as they often are, they assault my senses.

As Josh continues his tour, we eventually arrive at the master, with even this proving to be a monochromatic nightmare. I'm having trouble coming to terms with how different this is to the attic at The Daisy Chain.

Despite not caring one way or the other about football, I knew a lot were passionate about it. To be the reason that your team lost an important game could be devastating. Could him messing up his colors during that game, be the reason he's bleached all others from his life from thereon in?

As we stand at the end of the enormous bed, the only sports I can think of now are those involving Josh and me, naked. It must be something he picks up on, because next thing I know, we're on the bed in a glorious tangle of limbs.

Josh's lips sweep across mine while his hands range over my body, caressing me and tugging at my clothes. Not to be outdone, I'm as busy with my explorations. The sound of the zipper on his jeans was loud to my ears.

It's as if we're discovering each other all over again. Or is it loving him that has me feeling this way? At first, I'd thought my feelings toward him were down to him having saved my life. But this isn't it at all.

My fledgling love has grown with every second I'm with him. Heck, even when I'm not. He's gotten under my skin. My heart then stutters. What if he doesn't feel the same way? What if it's only physical for him?

With our relationship as new as it is, I can't even sound him out on it. At least not without coming across as a psychopath. And with the renovations at the Daisy Chain now on hold, I don't even have a reason to see him every day.

Next to me, Josh also stills, eventually propping himself up on one elbow. "Earth to Daisy, come in Daisy."

Now I'm torn. Much as I want to blurt out that I love him, simply to get it over with, the words don't come. I suspect I'd choke on them if I tried.

Rather, I panic, desperate to say something believable. Anything.

My relief when something comes to mind is immense. "I was just thinking I'll need to get myself sorted with temporary premises." While this was a throwaway line, soon enough, I realize it's a genuine concern. "I've got mortgage payments to make. And who knows how long before the renovations can start again?"

While the second part of my thought process was mostly said for my benefit, Josh responds anyway.

"Yeah, I was thinking about that. It won't be long before Ethan finds something else for us to do, but in the meantime, what do you think of... of setting up shop in my garage?"

For a moment, I can't respond. These aren't the actions of a man who doesn't want you to stick around. By working out of his garage, we'd see each other every day. But he's not finished yet, him taking a deep breath, a sure sign of that.

"And I thought maybe you could stay here?" He's quick to add, "But only if you want to."

Rather than answer in words, I squeal in delight, and then throw myself at him, rolling him onto his back and sitting astride him. The only thing wrong with this is that we're both still dressed.

It's something we soon take care of, and it's blissful. As smooth as Josh's skin sliding against mine are the sheets. While the color scheme might be utilitarian, the same can't be said for the linens.

The last time I slept on something this smooth was at a 5-star resort. The only difference is that today, there'll be no sleeping. It'll also be the first time we've made love in the cold light of day.

No flattering icicle lights, rather bright sunshine. And while this would have freaked me out in the past, the glint in Josh's eyes has me wanting to lay myself bare. To allow him to feast his eyes on my naked form, as I'm doing to him.

As he slowly inches inside me, his eyes dark with desire, I'm overcome. When he moves, the sunlight streaming through the window over the bed brings his colorful tattoos to life, and I can no longer hold back.

"Josh, I know it's early. But I ... I love you."

The tension in my body then mounts. Part of it because of the delicious waves radiating out from where our bodies join, part of it waiting on him to respond.

However, he says nothing. My heart shrinking as the rest of my body explodes, my nerve endings screaming their release as loudly as I am.

Despite being eaten alive by a climax that has all others paling, I watch Josh unsure if he'd heard me, or was simply pretending I hadn't spoken.

However, after shouting his own release, he collapses, holding me tight. "Daisy, I love you too. So much. And yeah, it is early days, but Daze, when you know, you know. And I know."

To be honest, after he'd told me he loved me, I had taken little notice of the rest of it, too busy focusing on my heart exploding with love.

Over the next few days, it's a wonder we achieve anything. We can't get enough of each other, with every time better than the last. Our lovemaking is now truly that, with the physical side not lessening one jot.

I'll never get sick of telling Josh that I love him. I'll never tire of him telling me the same. It adds dimension to our coupling that I'd thought only happened in movies or books.

In between our declarations of love, we've been busy ferrying all my tools of the trade from the end garage at The Laurels. While it'll be a squeeze compared to my old shop, I don't plan on having customers calling in here.

Rather, I'm going to concentrate on the commercial contracts that I'd let slip. Jobs where I can arrange the flowers here, before delivering them to clients. It's something I can even do with many of my regulars, with no end of queries about when I'll be back in business.

Despite it being nowhere near what I could make when set up properly, it'll be enough to cover costs if I'm careful. And with Josh and I rarely going out, I'm saving a fortune, with my life richer for it.

JOSH

Ethan has wasted no time getting another job lined up. It's one that will see me back at work after a delicious ten days at home with Daisy. Time spent setting her up in the garage and making love every chance we got.

On turning into the driveway after visiting the new site for a briefing, I'm surprised to see the roller door on the garage is down. Daisy's canary yellow 4x4 isn't parked in the driveway, telling me she must be out delivering arrangements.

I've not even got out of my truck when a beeping comes from behind me. There's nothing 'get out of my way, sucker' about it. Rather, it's a chirpy beep-beep that announces the love of my life.

We're soon in each other's arms, my lips finding hers in a kiss that promises so much more. However, she'll have none of it.

"I've got a few things I need your help with." After a final peck, she slides out of my arms and is off back down the driveway. It's only now that I see the back of her little 4x4 is packed to the roof.

"I thought you had everything you needed for the floral side of things?"

Her excitement is immediately tempered, with her even biting her bottom lip. I hate seeing her unsure of herself like this. And all thanks to the actions of that unscrupulous developer.

She's so different from the firecracker I'd first met.

Soon enough, my arms are full of large plastic trash bags that weigh next to nothing. It's only when I follow Daisy through the newly painted front door that I see what she's bought, although only after she's emptied all the bags.

On standing next to her and taking in the pile of cushions and throws, there's no missing that she's once again chewing her bottom lip. That all disappears after I scoop up a cushion and swat her playfully on the ass.

Not to be outdone, she returns the favor. While my intention hadn't been to have a pillow-fight, if this will have her smiling, then I'm all for it. It's something that soon sees us laughing on the couch, cocooned by all her purchases.

"They're only from the charity shop, but I thought ..." When she waves her hand around to take in the room, I don't allow her to say anything more.

"And you're absolutely right!"

We don't reference what we're talking about, with the lack of color in my home, something we've been studiously ignoring.

Daisy because she doesn't want to highlight my limitations, and me because I don't want her to feel guilty about being able to see color. The elephant in the room is both gray or bursting with color, depending on your viewpoint.

Despite their humble origins, the new-to-us furnishings make an enormous difference, even to my jaded eyes. The one surprise for me is Daisy's fondness for green.

Our days of playing house are over all too soon. Daisy is once again busy with corporate clients and arranging flowers for weddings.

Meanwhile, I'm working on the office upgrade in town that Ethan had secured. It wasn't something he'd usually go for. However, everyone on the team is happy about the income.

The charges against the dirty property developer look like they'll stick. This is especially so with more and more people coming out of the woodwork, accusing him of similar acts. The last I heard was that investors were abandoning him like rats leaving a sinking ship.

It was for this reason many a sale had fallen through, with the business owners more than happy about this. I'd even seen that the dry cleaner next to The Daisy Chain was back up and running.

As the weeks progress, Daisy and I fall into a comfortable routine, happy in our skin and even happier with each other. And yet there's a shadow hanging over her head. One she does her best to ignore. More than that, it's as if she's pretending the building isn't even hers anymore.

The fire has definitely taken the shine off the Victorian, and I think she's happy the renovations are on hold. I honestly think if it wasn't for the pending court case, she'd have sold the place by now.

And probably for a lot less than she'd paid for it. But I'll not let her lose money like that, not while I'm capable of doing something about it.

More than that, part of me wants her to love the building as much as I love her. It was why I'd been getting home late for weeks, telling Daisy the latest project was bigger than Texas. I'd even worked the occasional weekend when I knew she'd be tied up with her own business.

And as busy as she'd been with this, she hadn't questioned me. Not once.

Despite all the extra hours, it was slow going, although this soon enough changed. When the others on the team had found out what I was up to, they'd offered to help.

It still took four months to effect the changes. Four months of lying to the woman I love, of being sneaky. It's taken long enough that I'm nervous, worried she'll think I'm up to no good.

And while this is true, it isn't anything that would hurt her. I only have to keep up the pretense for three more days.

"Daisy, can you take this Saturday afternoon off?"

I've kept my tone as light as I can, and yet she still picks up that something is wrong, albeit not in the way she's obviously thinking.

. . .

Saturday afternoon, sees me helping her up into the cab of my truck. However, rather than reverse out onto the road, I hold up a sleep mask. "You'll need to put this on. It's a surprise."

For a start, I think she's going to balk at doing so, although after grinning, she does as I've asked. Rather than drive straight to The Daisy Chain, I take a circuitous route, hoping to throw her off the scent.

It sure does that, with her constantly asking where we're going. Soon enough, I park outside The Daisy Chain, the old building gleaming thanks to a fresh coat of white paint.

And no, this wasn't because of my dodgy eyesight, but because the lady at Tremaine's told me it was the correct color for a building of this age. After helping Daisy out of the truck and onto the sidewalk, I take a deep breath.

"Okay, you can remove it now."

She's slow to comply, suddenly nervous. Eventually, though, she slides it up and over her forehead, blinking rapidly, her confusion clear.

DAISY

The last time I'd seen The Daisy Chain, the paint on the siding was peeling and the front windows were boarded up. In stark contrast, the paintwork now gleams, while the rippled glass in the front windows sparkles in the sunlight.

I walk forward, reaching out, and running my fingers down the panes one after the other, before turning to look at Josh. "But how?" I'm so confused. I'd seen those windows destroyed, and the glazier had said it was impossible to replace like with like.

Josh shrugs as if it was nothing, his words immediately making a lie of this. "Yeah, replacing those was a bit of a mission. I had to scour demo yards all over town to find the right vintage glass. Then I got Zac Thomas, you remember him, to replicate the original frames."

It's only when my cheeks prickle, I realize I'm crying, although I'm quick to assert, "They're happy tears!"

However, the surprises aren't over yet.

One arm slung around my shoulders, he steers me over to the front doors and puts a key in the lock. After opening the double doors wide, he urges me to walk in ahead of him.

I only manage a couple of steps before I'm again unable to move. When I'd left here all those months back, the shop was full of smoke, and there'd been water from the tank pooled everywhere. It had been miserable, much like me.

On looking up, I see my old sign mounted on the wall above the counter. It's perfect, a lot like the shop itself. Gone are the washed-out hues that had faded thanks to sunshine and time.

They've been replaced by a riot of color, a surprise given Josh's involvement.

Again, I'm thrown. A glance at Josh, and I'm unable to stop myself from whispering, "You?" I've seen how wrong he can get colors, and yet the palette he's used is glorious.

"I might have had a little help."

On me arching an eyebrow, he spills the beans. Whoever that lady at Tremaine's Hardware was, I owe her big time.

Still, him having chosen everything from a special-edition collection had made it harder for him to go wrong. Despite all this, I'm thrilled with the overall effect.

"Is it okay? Do you like it?"

There's no missing the trepidation in his voice. While my rough-and-ready research said people with red/green colorblindness often see blues clearly, other colors can lack vibrancy. Then, as if seeing the shop through his eyes, I'm hit by a wave of sadness.

As so often happens these days, I throw myself into his arms, with him catching me. "Oh Josh, I love it. I love it almost as much as I love you."

After kissing me senseless, he lets me slide down the front of his body, letting me know he's a happy camper. Another quick kiss and he turns and locks the front doors. We'll not be disturbed now.

"How about I show you the rest of it, and how much I love you while we're about it?"

There's no missing his message and after a squeal, followed by a giggle, I dance backward, leaving him to follow as best he can. Any thoughts of escape flee the moment I spin joyously into the small hallway and face the main stairs.

The last time I'd seen them, the balustrade was black and the carpet runner had been steaming. When I'd tottered down them after being saved by the firefighters, I swore to myself that I'd never use them again.

It's for this reason I head for the kitchen, not expecting to see much difference. The original renovation had always been about getting the shop ready to open, with everything else on the back burner.

One look at the back burner on the ancient range and I know Josh has gone way beyond getting the shop tidied up. The kitchen and dining area are immaculate, looking as they must have when the building was new.

Unlike the shop, the colors in here are muted, a lot like Josh when he stops next to me. There's no missing that he's on edge, although I'm unsure why. He's played it safe in here.

Then it hits me. If he's taken the renovations this far, then he's surely expecting me to move out of his place. And just like that, the colors that had until now delighted me, are as lackluster as my spirit.

As if noticing the change in me, Josh's gaze darts around as if looking for faults. "You don't like it?" When I don't immediately assure him, he presses on. "If you don't like something, I can change it. I just want you to be happy, Daze."

I have to ask. If I don't, I'll kick myself. Too often, I've stayed quiet, then been left to wonder how different my life could have been if I'd only asked.

"Josh." While it's a start, it's nowhere near enough for him to go on. After drawing in as much air as my emotions will allow, I burst out with, "Do you want me to move out of your place?" My question has been rushed, the words tumbling over each other in my panic to be free of them.

My eyes were now locked on the newly polished floorboards, with me scared to read the answer in his eyes. I knew things had moved too quickly between us, even if that wasn't how it had felt to me.

Never have I felt as comfortable with a man. Every moment I'm with him, I'm at peace. Although not right now.

All that changes when Josh puts his finger under my chin and tips my head back. There's no avoiding his gaze now. As I stare up at him, I'm conscious of my pulse thundering in my throat as I desperately look for unspoken clues.

Josh doesn't give me time, dragging me hard against his chest with his free hand, his lips smashing into mine in a kiss that sears and claims me as his.

And even though his kiss has given me the answer I'm desperate for, I still want to hear him say it. Just because he's always telling me he loves me, that doesn't mean he wants to live with me full-time.

"Daze, for an intelligent woman, you can be awfully stupid." I'd be insulted, but for the curl of his lips and the twinkle in his eyes. "No, I don't want you to move out, it's just that ..."

Before I have time to freak out completely, he continues, "I was just thinking there's more room here."

Is he saying what I think he's saying?

"You don't need to answer me now. And I'll even be okay if you want to sell it. At least you'll get a decent price with it done up."

Darn it, I hate seeing him looking unsure of himself like this. He's had too much of this in his life. "I guess it will depend, Josh."

While I then do my best to keep a straight face, I fail miserably, with my lips quirking up of their own volition. It's hard to hide a smile when all you want to do is laugh and grin like a loon.

JOSH

For someone who said they never wanted to step foot in that attic again, Daisy is wasting no time getting up there. I just hope she likes what I've done with the place.

The changes are obvious right from the moment you turn the corner in the hallway. First off, the sliding panel is no longer there, although I'm not telling Daisy this is because it was so badly damaged.

The other change I'd made is that the previously hidden staircase is now wider and the treads regulation depth. While grandpa and me might have skirted the law when building our hidden version, it wasn't something I could get away with now. That guy from the planning department was a pain in the ass with making sure we followed the rules.

On stepping up into the attic, I find Daisy rooted to the spot, busy taking everything in. It's nothing like it was when she was last here. It's much improved, with the narrow iron bed having been replaced by a king size beauty with a padded headboard.

I know when she spots the sprinkler system, thanks to her gasping and even pointing.

The other addition is the icicle lights have been replaced by thousands of safer modern equivalents, although they're hard to spot in the daylight. Just because the old school version hadn't started the fire that night, that doesn't mean they weren't capable of it. Those little suckers got hot.

Memories of the fire have me steering Daisy over to the windows. As I'd done in the shop below, the smashed central pane has been replaced with another vintage find.

As she'd done downstairs, she reaches out and runs her fingers down the pane, before turning and giving me a smile that lights up her face.

"Did you see what's outside? Check the sash windows."

This has her putting in as much effort to open the window on her side as she had the night of the fire. However, this time, the window shoots up with a loud clatter. A moment later and she's hanging out of it, with more exclamations of delight following.

Never would I forget us standing huddled next to that smashed window, desperately sucking in fresh air. It was for this reason a proper fire escape had been at the top of my list.

I know all my precautions might be over the top, but I never wanted to be caught like that again. I won't risk Daisy's life. I don't want to risk what we've got. She's not out there for long, pulling her head back inside the room and smiling at me.

She's not ready to settle though, walking about the space, taking in all the changes I've made. When she stops in front of the bookcase with all my toys back on display, my breath stalls.

I'm not sure how she'll feel about me leaving my childhood memorabilia here. It's her home now, not mine. For all I wish it was otherwise. Daisy gently reaches out and tentatively pokes my old football before picking it up. Like a lot of things in the attic, it's in better shape than the last time she saw it.

Gone is the knife I'd stabbed it with the day I'd been kicked off the team. "I decided that rather than bury the knife, it was time to bury the past."

She nods in agreement before putting the football back on the top shelf.

Soon enough, Daisy runs out of things to look at. The only thing she hasn't truly examined is the enormous bed, even if there's no missing the beast. While it had been fun sharing the narrow cot with her, it had its limitations.

And as difficult as it had been getting the monster mattress up here, I'm keen to try it out. "It's memory foam."

It's enough to break Daisy's concentration, with her looking away from the new drywall that hides where the old water tank had been. It doesn't matter that it had saved our lives. The fewer reminders we have of the fire, the better.

Despite there now being no outward signs, there's still a sadness in her eyes that I long to get rid of. This has me walking over and holding her tight. "I was just saying the mattress is memory foam."

However, I leave it there, not wanting to push it. While there are no limitations on how close we are back at my place, I don't want lousy memories ruining it for us here.

I also like to think we've got plenty of time to erase those and start afresh. The building had always rung with laughter when my grandparents lived here, and I liked to think it could be like that again.

"Do you want to check out the bathroom downstairs?"

She looks up at me, obviously thrown by this change in direction.

"I've installed a monster water heater. We can fill that thing to the brim."

At last I see something in her eyes that promises a good time for both of us, and after stepping back, I hold my hand out.

The closer we get to the bathroom, the more nervous I am. While I'd played it safe everywhere else, the smallest room in the house is another story. What if I got it wrong? What if she hates it?

This has my heart firmly lodged in my mouth when I open the door and step to the side. Sure, I want to know if she loves it. But if she hates it, I'm not sure what I'll do. Rip all the tiles down and start afresh, I guess.

I'm still going through the logistics of this, and how quickly I can affect it, when there's a squeal from inside the bathroom. It hadn't sounded like one of distress to me.

After squaring my shoulders, I join her, relieved to see her eyes alight with laughter and a huge grin splitting her face. "I love it, Josh. I just love it."

Next thing I know, she's put the plug in the bath and has turned the faucets on as far as they'll go, with steam soon filling the room. When I see how quickly she's shedding her clothes, I give up thinking it through and instead I go with it.

Or rather, I go with her.

On sinking into the water and her laying back against my chest, all is right with my world. "Damn, this feels good." I swish my hands around her sides and cup her breasts, her nipples puckering in response to my touch. "You feel good."

The Josh of old would have choked on the words he was looking for. With Daisy in my life, that man is gone. Just as my colorblindness had robbed me of my confidence in the past, Daisy has given it back to me.

"I love you, Daisy Green. I can't imagine my life without you. You color my world."

I then lower my lips to the back of her neck, kissing it reverently. Never could I have imagined all those months back when I was existing rather than living, that life could be this good.

After deliberately grinding her ass into my erection, Daisy turns her head to the side and looks at me over her shoulder. "Just as I love you, Josh Kendrick." Then, with a sleight of hand that has me gasping, she slides her hand behind her back, gripping me tight.

"Woman, if you keep that up, we'll flood the bathroom."

She giggles, not loosening her grip. "I don't care, Josh. I'm used to being wet when you're around."

EPILOGUE
FIRST CHRISTMAS TOGETHER

DAISY

Christmas Eve finds me in the front room on the second-floor, finishing up the decorations on the tree. As I tinker with the baubles and ribbons, nervous excitement bubbles up inside of me. While outwardly, everything is uniformly silver, there are hidden depths to this tree.

Just how hidden, or not, will depend if the gift I've bought Josh works out as I hope. There'd been a lot of underhanded plans involved in getting it just right, and even then, it wasn't guaranteed it would work. The website even warned of this.

Much as it would have been lovely to have the large tree up in the attic, it was impossible thanks to the confines of the stairwell. The other reason was that so often when we were up in the attic, we only had eyes for each other, with our passion blinding us to all else.

Better we have it in our official front parlor and the place we spend most evenings after dinner, and somewhere we can enjoy its festive cheer.

Despite Josh saying I was welcome to stay at his place, it hadn't worked out that way. And after I'd moved all my work tools to The Daisy Chain, it'd made no sense.

Add to this that the bed he'd struggled to install in the attic was bigger and more comfortable than his, or even mine, and we were sold.

It had only been a matter of weeks before Josh was living with me above The Daisy Chain and he had installed tenants in his place. While some thought it was rushed, to us it felt natural and so very right.

I loved waking up next to Josh in the morning, as I loved falling asleep in his arms after we'd made love in the evening.

The last thing I do before going downstairs to join him for dinner is to grab a brightly wrapped box out of the sideboard and slide it under the tree. If it weren't for this, I'd never have seen the large dark green box tucked away there. The one with my name on it. Tempting as it is to pick it up and shake it, I leave it where it is.

I'll soon find out what he's bought me, with us set to open our presents after dinner, as had been the custom with Josh's grandparents. And with their presence in the building a constant, it made sense to us to continue the tradition.

On plodding back up the stairs to the parlor after dinner, I'm sure I'm about to burst with anticipation and from having eaten too much. On hearing Josh groaning next to me, I doubt I'm alone.

"I think I ate too much." Actually, there's no 'think' about it, with me glad I'm wearing my brightly colored Christmas dress and not jeans and a sweater.

"I'm with you on that front." Josh follows this up by undoing his belt and simply letting the buckle and tail hang free.

As tempting as it is to make the most of this and see Christmas in with a bang, I hold myself back. Much as I want to make love to Josh, I want to see what he thinks of my gift first.

If it all goes horribly wrong, then at least I know how I'll distract him.

Only once cognacs have been poured do I hunker down next to the tree and retrieve Josh's present. I then hand it to him reverently and join him on the couch.

He looks askance at me, his brow knotted. "I thought we agreed that we'd only get each other something little." He holds the box up, twisting it first one way, and then the other. "Why is my gut telling me there's nothing little about this?"

Despite me doing my best to clear my face of all emotion, I know I've failed when he slowly shakes his head.

"Come on, Josh. Open it!"

While I'm itching to take it off him and rip the paper to shreds, I hold myself back, silently screaming in anticipation as he takes his own sweet time.

In double the time it would have taken me, he's removed the paper to reveal a nondescript box. He's as slow to open this, and when he sees that it's a pair of sunglasses, his reaction is underwhelming.

A quick look around the room and I realize the lighting is far too subdued for him to notice the effects of the glasses. After standing as quickly as my overstuffed tummy will allow, I flick on all the lights.

"Go on, try them on."

Now he's looking at me as though I've lost it, which I will if he doesn't put those darn glasses on. After yet another strange look at me, he slides them on, with him then looking at me as if to say, "Now what?"

He doesn't stay like that for long, with him ripping the glasses off and again looking at me. Soon after, he slams them back on his face.

This time he keeps them on a little longer, although he eventually has to remove them to wipe his tears. "Is this truly how you see the world?"

I nod tentatively, not knowing if what he's currently seeing is what I see every day. All I can tell from his reaction is that whatever it is, it's emotionally overwhelming.

A second later, he's got the glasses back on and is holding his arms out and yelling. "My tattoos! Freaking, look at my tattoos!" After turning his arms this way and that, he again looks at me, his bewilderment clear.

"I always thought they were just blues and greens. I didn't realize there were ... reds in there, too. I just told the guy to use whatever colors he wanted."

His reaction to seeing the actual colors of the tattoos that snake up both his arms soon pales when I hit the remote in my pocket.

The multi-colored lights hidden in the depths of the Christmas Tree burst into life, with Josh's expression more than I could have hoped for. Then, despite my telling him to keep them on, that his eyes needed time to adjust, he removed the glasses, putting them down carefully on the coffee table.

A second later and I'm in his arms, able to taste his tears when I kiss him.

Could I truly love this wonderful man any more than I already do?

Apparently so.

JOSH

There's nothing I can do to stop myself from staring around the room open mouthed, my senses in freefall. I can't decide what to look at next.

The riotous paper Daisy wrapped the ChromaMax glasses in, her festive dress, or the Christmas Tree dancing with color in the corner?

In the end, I decide I don't have to choose, because I'm never taking these glasses off, like ever. I come back to earth with a bump when I realize the gift that I'd gotten Daisy can't compare. At least not in my eyes.

I know she knows it's under the tree simply by how often her gaze drifts in that direction before returning to me. When I was arranging it, I thought it was the best gift idea ever.

Now I've got close-to-normal eyesight, I'm no longer as sure. However, I know I'll have to give it to her, anyway. Better a hideous gift than no gift at all.

And with me now wanting it over and done with, I'm soon down on my hands and knees, reaching under the lower branches, and sliding the large box free.

It doesn't matter that I've got my back to her, with me easily able to hear Daisy's gasp of breath. However, I don't think it's got anything to do with the present.

Hell, she's told me often enough how much she likes my ass. It's something I'll use as a distraction if she's appalled by the most visual part of my gift. After getting her to move our cognacs to one side, I place the large box on the coffee table.

"All you need to do is lift the lid." Instructions handed over, I grab my cognac and sit back on the couch. A second later, and my drink is gone, with me then reaching out and grabbing hers.

She's therefore looking at me and not the gift when she slides the lid free. However, when she drops it next to the coffee table and turns to see what's inside, she's struck dumb.

And so am I. I'm looking at the bouquet housed in the special box with as much awe as she is. When I'd gotten out of bed at four this morning to create it, I wasn't able to see the true colors of the blooms I was working with.

Rather, I'd stuck to the colors that I thought Daisy liked. My fingers crossed that these at least would go together, even if they looked all kinds of wrong to me. Fortunately, the bouquet, while blinding in its intensity, works so well, especially when viewed through the ChromaMax glasses.

Daisy reaches into the box and pulls the bouquet free, complete with the cardboard vase I'd helped myself to out of her supplies. Obviously, I'd learned a thing or two after watching her complete many a bouquet.

It's only when I see she's looking to be supremely pissed that I realize something. Hah, she thinks I got it from one of the other florists in town. While I might be a simple man who works in construction, even I'm not that stupid.

"Relax, will you? I got up and put it together this morning."

There's no missing that she doesn't believe me, despite my never having lied to her. However, I know of a quick way to prove I was behind the arrangement. After taking it off her, I yank the flowers free of the cardboard box. Perhaps a little too roughly, with her sucking in air in response to my handling of the precious blooms.

However, when she sees the bouquet is held together with a couple of zip ties, with me unable to work with that string she prefers, her ire melts. I'm not finished yet, though.

I want this moment to be perfect, which has me placing the bouquet back in its cardboard vase. I'll need my hands free for what comes next. Not giving Daisy a chance to so much as move, I slide my hand into the very heart of the arrangement.

It's here I find the small box I'd hidden earlier, the contents of which have the power to change both our lives. Then, in a move I might have practiced, I pull the small box free, flip the lid and slide onto one knee on the floor.

It's smooth. The only thing not smooth is my heartbeat, with it hammering as hard as I do during demo. And Daisy staring at me open-mouthed, stunned, her face devoid of emotion, doesn't have it slowing any.

Damn it, this isn't looking good.

I'm still thinking I've somehow screwed up when she launches herself at me, sending us both into a heap on the floor.

"Yes! My answer is yes!"

Later that night, I'm still coming to terms with how wonderful my new, more colorful life is. The woman I love is wrapped tight around my length, with her keening telling me she loves my second Christmas present just as much as the first.

I savor the moment for as long as I can until surrendering to a climax that's every bit as strong as hers apparently had been. "Oh God, I love you, Daze. So, so much."

It wasn't until this wonderful woman became part of my life that I'd realized how lacking in color it was. And this went further than my colorblindness. With Daisy beside me, I laugh more, and my life is brighter all round.

After sinking into the mattress, she rests her head on my chest, her hair, as always, tickling my nose. "Daisy, you color my world."

She lifts her head and looks me dead in the eye. "And without you in my life, my world was gray."

As we fall asleep, I know my life will never be the same, and I have this gorgeous creature to thank for that.

THANK YOU

If you've enjoyed this book, I'd be thrilled if you could take the time to rate or review it either on the site where you purchased it, or on your favorite review site.

Meet the gorgeous, talented crew from **Lucky Break Construction**, whose motto should read *"If we build it, you will come!"* because apparently a few of Coogan's Break single ladies have done just that.

If you've enjoyed your time in Coogan's Break, consider staying a while, by treating yourself to the large format six packs of books 1-6 and 7-12. Available from all good online retailers.

Written in British English, this humorous (not a typo) series is full of bad language, bad behaviour (still not a typo) and poorly executed Farrah Fawcett hairstyles.

It also touches on the real life issues facing women at that time, which can make the books raw in places. Isn't it time you transported yourself back to the craziest of decades?

Available from all good online retailers.

MARINA WITCHES
COZY MYSTERY SERIES

ANDIE LOW

Frankie's a jinxed witch with Bruce Lee moves.
Dex is her snarky Jack Russell. Together with Zane,
Frankie's drop-dead gorgeous, neighbor,
these three are magic.

Left in charge of her grandmother's marriage agency, vampire matchmaker, Eva De Silva, is expecting a peaceful gig. She's wrong.

On her first night, she gets hit with unexpected visitors, a dangerous family relic goes missing, and she's framed for murder. Luckily, she has Dominik Zilonka—her newest client and vampire voted least likely to settle down—on hand to help.

Eva must stay sharp to save the business, clear her name, and find Dominik a wife, all while ignoring that she's his perfect blood bond.

* 9 7 8 1 7 3 8 6 0 6 8 1 8 *